W9-ADR-306

WITHDRAWN

HIS INDIAN BROTHER

HIS INDIAN BROTHER

HAZEL WILSON

Illustrated by Robert Henneberger

60768

ABINGDON PRESS
New York • Nashville

Cody Memorial Library
Southwestern University
Georgetown, Texas

Copyright 1955 by Pierce and Washabaugh

All rights reserved

Printed in the United States of America

B

THIS BOOK IS AFFECTIONATELY DEDICATED TO MY SISTER

Marion

WHO WENT WITH ME TO VISIT THE PENOBSCOT INDIANS

CF
W693h

10-13-56 Purch. Gift (250

Contents

1	Up River	11
2	Working Together	18
3	Alone	29
4	Lost	41
5	Waiting	58
6	The Bear in the Canoe	69
7	Their Daily Bread	83
8	The Bough House	94
9	The Honey Tree	104
10	Escape	116

11   *Fire!*   129

12   *To Run with the Moose*   141

13   *Chief Kineowa Returns*   152

14   *Together Again*   165

15   *Between Two Magnets*   173

     AUTHOR'S NOTE   187

HIS INDIAN BROTHER

Brad and his father paddled steadily up the Penobscot River

1

Up River

"It's May Day by the almanac today," said Mr. Porter, not breaking the rhythm of his steady paddling. "Feels more like the first of March up here in the Maine woods."

Brad saw traces of snow in the hollows between the pines along the riverbank. "Guess the District of Maine doesn't know it's spring," he said, keeping his paddle strokes in time with his father's.

It was late afternoon of the third day of their journey up the Penobscot River from the Indian village of Old Town. It seemed to Brad that their canoe had come all of a hundred miles, yet his father said it was less than fifty. Paddling against the current made it seem longer. Brad's muscles had their usual afternoon ache, though it

11

was not the intense pain he had felt toward the end of the first day.

"I don't mind it so much now that the blisters on my hands are becoming calluses," Brad told his father.

"I said you'd harden up if you kept at it," remarked Mr. Porter.

"Aren't we most there, Pa? Are you sure we haven't gone by our land?"

"Of course I'm sure. I judge we're almost there. Watch on the right for a high ledge set back from the river, with a stand of white birches just below it. According to my chart, my land's around the next bend. Should see the ledge any minute now."

As Brad's arms continued the constant dip and lift of his paddle, his eyes searched the riverbank. He saw no sign of high ledge or birches. There was not a break in the dense forest of evergreens.

It was the year 1809, and the shipbuilding trade had been ruined in Boston because of the embargo on shipping. So Mr. Porter, who had been a master shipbuilder, had bought a tract of wild land in Maine. He and thirteen-year-old Brad were on their way there to clear land and build a cabin. Then Mr. Porter would return to Boston for the rest of the family, leaving Brad to look after their new home.

All the way up river, thoughts of how it would be

while he waited alone for the family had been in Brad's mind. Sometimes he was afraid he would be lonely and scared. Sometimes he was thrilled at the prospect of being his own master.

He saw something moving behind the trees. It could be a deer. It might be an Indian. Brad knew that tribes of Penobscot Indians still lived somewhere in the woods up here, though he and his father had not seen an Indian since they had left Old Town.

"Pa," said Brad worriedly, "are you dead sure the Indians won't drive us away? Remember that big Indian who kept yelling at us while we were loading the canoe? He kept saying, 'White man stay out of Indian country. All land up river belong to Indians.'"

"He was drunk," said Mr. Porter. "He wouldn't have talked that way if he'd been sober. I've told you time and time again that Maine's had no trouble with the Indians for years. They agreed by treaty to open up part of the land up river for settlement. I've bought and paid for my land and have the deed in my pocket to prove it. Nobody's going to drive us away. You don't need to worry about Indians."

Brad knew his father's words were true, yet he could not rid himself of an uneasy feeling about Indians.

"I'm glad Pa's leaving his rifle with me," he told himself. "Then if I have to defend myself against Indians, I can. Of course I won't have to, but if I did, I could."

He saw a raccoon and her four babies come out of the woods. The black on their faces gave them a comic look. Then he looked ahead and saw a high wall of granite set back from the river. The late afternoon sunshine slanted against the silken white of birches at the base of the ledge.

"We're there!" Brad cried. "See the ledge, Pa? We're coming to the bend. Is all the land beyond it ours?"

"Three hundred acres of it is," said Brad's father, pride of ownership in his voice.

They rounded the bend and saw endless lines of evergreens, growing so close together their branches interlocked.

"I hope I'm doing the right thing, moving to this wilderness," Mr. Porter said as they landed the canoe and lifted it on shore. "By the looks, not a soul has been here since creation."

The thought of being the first human being to step on this riverbank pleased Brad. He knew the land had been surveyed only roughly and that it was possible nobody had been here before. He and his father were explorers, Brad thought. Even a little like the Pilgrims. They had been the first settlers in Massachusetts, but surely he and Pa were the first settlers in this part of the District of Maine.

14

"Thank God we got here alive," said Brad's father, getting out two long-handled axes which had been tied to a roll of blankets.

Brad remembered hearing that when, nearly two hundred years ago, the Pilgrims had landed, they had knelt down and given thanks for their safe voyage. His father was not kneeling but what he had said was a sort of prayer, Brad decided. "We're really something like the Pilgrims," Brad said aloud.

"What? Guess in a way we are. Only across the ocean was a sight farther off from civilization than fifty-odd miles up river. Take an ax, Brad, and cut up some wood. There's no real hurry about that, though. Tell you what, we'll celebrate our arrival by going fishing. I'd relish a good mess of fried fish for supper. We were in too much of a hurry to get here to stop and fish along the way. Where did you pack the fishing tackle, Brad?"

Brad fumbled with the cord that bound one of the gunny sacks. Then he had a sudden hollow feeling at the pit of his stomach. He looked at his father with a stricken look in his gray eyes. "I forgot to pack the fishing tackle," he confessed in a low voice. "I was going out to the shed to get the box of hooks when Ma asked me to go to the store. Then it slipped my mind. Honest, I didn't mean to forget."

"A lot of good that does," said his father harshly.

15

"Sometimes I believe you'd forget your head if it wasn't hitched on. Brad," he said more kindly but with great earnestness, "your forgetting to pack the fishing tackle after I distinctly asked you to is no life or death matter. You can live without fish until I return from Boston, for I'm leaving you plenty to eat. But you must realize how important it is up here not to be forgetful. Nature doesn't excuse forgetfulness or carelessness. You *have* to be careful. You can't afford to forget. If you do, you may be a goner. I'm really worried about leaving you up here by yourself. I really am. Perhaps it would be better for you to go back with me after we get the cabin built."

It seemed to Brad that his father was being pretty hard on him because of one instant of forgetfulness. "But, Pa, you said somebody should stay up here and look out for things. You said you wanted me to go on getting the place ready for Ma and the twins while you were gone." It suddenly seemed the most important thing in the world to Brad to be thought capable of being left in charge of the yet unbuilt cabin.

"We'll see," said his father dryly. "Now go get some wood." He sniffed the air and a gentle look came over his face. "I smell Mayflowers," he said. He knelt and picked a few sprays of faintly pink trailing arbutus from the midst of clumps of ground pine. "Your mother will be real pleased that Mayflowers grow up here," he said.

16

"Ma loves flowers all right," said Brad, glad to have the subject changed from his shortcomings. "So do Prudy and Trudy. Think the twins will like it way up here in the woods?" He thought of his seven-year-old sisters, blonde and rosy and as alike as two peas in a pod.

"Like it? Of course they will," said Mr. Porter firmly. "Why shouldn't they? This is our new home." And he looked at the forest with eyes unafraid of its vastness.

"I already like it better than Boston," said Brad, cheerful again. He whistled as he picked up an ax and went off to find a dead tree small enough to cut down without much work.

"We're here, and this neck of the woods is all ours," he thought as he chopped. "I'm breathing Porter air, and all the pine trees that make it smell so good are ours."

Brad, too, had begun to enjoy a feeling of ownership.

2

Working Together

The next day the woods rang with the sound of chopping as Brad and his father attacked the trees with their long-handled axes. The spot Mr. Porter had chosen for a cabin was on the rise of a gentle slope about a hundred feet from the river. All the dense growth of pine and spruce on it had to be cut.

"We're the first men to make an opening in the woods at this place," Mr. Porter told Brad as they chopped at opposite sides of a giant pine.

Brad flushed with pleasure at being counted a man. He tried to put more force into the blows of his ax. At one mighty swing he missed the tree and, cutting only thin air, all but fell on his face.

"Slow and steady does it," said his father, not unkindly.

Chop, chop, chop. Brad's eye traveled up the tree trunk and he saw the shape of an arrow cut deep in the wood. "Look, Pa," he said, pointing.

"Well," said Mr. Porter, "this is the first tree I've ever seen marked with the king's arrow. When this country was a colony, men were sent into the woods to mark the tallest pines to be saved for ships of the British navy. This must have been a fine tree years ago. It's a giant now. Seems almost a pity to cut it down."

"Then we aren't the first people who have ever been in these woods after all," said Brad, disappointed.

Mr. Porter made the chips fly. "Others may have passed by here but we'll be the first to stay," he said.

Chop, chop, chop. A person became just as tired chopping down a tree as paddling a canoe, Brad decided after half an hour. He envied his father's strong muscles. His arms were still spindly. Brad wished he had grown stocky the past year instead of merely lengthening.

Chop, chop, chop. This tree was as tough as all get out. Its trunk did not so much as quiver after all this hacking at it. The morning was chilly, yet sweat poured down Brad's face. He stopped work long enough to peel off his shirt.

"Take a few minutes off," advised his father. "It will

19

be some time before we get the best of this big fellow. I don't mind working awhile alone."

Brad put down his ax. He had always found it easier to stop than to begin work. Now he would have a chance to explore his new surroundings. He had been too weary the night before to do more than eat his supper and roll up in his blanket and go to sleep.

There was a springiness to the ground underfoot, where generations of pine needles had fallen. Pools of water and traces of snow were in the hollows. It was rough, rocky, thickly wooded land, about as different from the city of Boston where he had been born and brought up as a place could be. Instead of hurrying people, there were scurrying small wild animals. Brad caught glimpses of woodchucks, squirrels, a skunk, and what he thought was a wildcat. He saw and smelled a fox. A young deer came so close that Brad looked into his eyes before fear grew in them and the graceful animal leaped away.

Brad knew there were fiercer animals than these in the woods. When he and his father had camped at night on the trip up the Penobscot, he had heard wolves howl. One night a bear had trotted up to the campfire but had quickly gone away. Brad had not been afraid of wild animals with his father there with a ready rifle.

"After Pa goes and I'm up here by myself, I won't be afraid, either," he thought. "For I can scare anything away with Pa's rifle. Even Indians. And I hope I'll get in some days of good hunting."

"Brad! Brad!" called his father.

"Back to the grindstone," sighed Brad, turning toward the sound of his father's chopping.

As Brad crashed through the underbrush, he looked up and suddenly saw the great top of the pine shake. He heard a sharp rending of wood. His terrified eyes saw the giant tree falling directly at him. He leaped to one side. Then slashing branches struck him to the ground and fairly beat the breath out of him.

His father ran to pull him out from under the tangle of branches. "Are you all right? Can you stand? Can you walk? Thank God the trunk missed you!"

"Why didn't you tell me the tree was about to fall?" complained Brad. He wiped a trickle of blood from his scratched face. "Guess I'm all right. Still a little shaky."

"I didn't know the tree had a hollow heart," said Mr. Porter. "When my ax bit into it, the trunk snapped like a toothpick. I didn't have a minute's warning."

"I saw the top shake and I never jumped faster." Brad was proud of having acted so quickly.

"And a good thing you did," approved his father. "Now sit and get your breath back and then grub out some of this underbrush."

Brad sighed. Apparently even having nearly been

21

killed was not going to make his father excuse him from working.

It took a week to clear the cabin site and several more days to burn the stumps and pry them loose. The roots had to be chopped close to each stump before it could be lifted with a crowbar and plenty of elbow grease. Brad was reminded of yanking out teeth. Only the stump teeth were never loose. Brad grew very tired of stumps before the ground for the cabin was cleared.

He enjoyed helping build the cabin. He and his father kept at it, rain or shine. Mr. Porter took the same pains building his cabin as he had with a ship. He chose the logs carefully and notched them exactly right to fit at the corners. He and Brad put the cabin together solidly, to last.

The day they put on the roof, Brad noticed the first green in the grass along the riverbank and saw buds at the ends of the branches of the evergreens. Spring was building, too, along with the cabin. Getting the roof on was a time of worry, work, and, at last, triumph. When it was done, Brad and his father stood and surveyed their handiwork with pride. "It's a satisfaction to a man to build shelter for his family with his own hands," said Mr. Porter. "And you helped, Brad. I don't know what I would have done without you."

His father's praise made Brad feel inches taller and as strong as an ox — at least a small one.

"Guess it does take two to raise a roof," Brad said gruffly.

It seemed strange that night to be sleeping with a roof over his head again. He missed having a clear view of the stars. Yet Brad remembered that on cold, rainy nights he had been miserable. And he was glad to be out of reach of the wind, which had a bite to it even well along in the month of May.

By the end of the third week, Mr. Porter was ready to go back to Boston. The morning of his departure, he and Brad were up at dawn, for he wanted to get an early start. Before Brad was awake, his father had built a fire in the stone fireplace they had finished making only two days ago. Now they were sitting on a crude bench before the fire, eating a hurried breakfast of cornmeal mush and molasses.

"I'm sorry I didn't have time to build the chimney," said Mr. Porter. He looked up at the chimney hole in the roof through which sparks and smoke were rising. "Remember it's not safe to have too hot a fire."

"Yes, Pa."

"When you're gathering stones for the chimney, try to get them pretty much the same size."

"Yes, Pa."

"We'll get at the chimney first thing when I get back," said Mr. Porter. "Wish we could have gotten out the stumps from the patch of land we cleared for the garden. That's too hard for you to do by yourself. Just plant the potatoes and corn between the stumps. Better get at it today."

"Yes, Pa."

"I hope you get around to walling up the spring back of the cabin," said Mr. Porter. "Your mother will use river water for everything but drinking. But nothing is as good

24

to drink as clear, cold spring water. Oh, and Brad, don't forget to chink the logs with clay in your spare time. I've done the roof but you can still see daylight through the cracks in the cabin walls."

Brad sighed. Being reminded of so many things to do made him tired before he started doing any of them. "I'd hoped to get in a little time for hunting," he said. "You told me I would have to get most of my meat by shooting it."

"No reason why you shouldn't shoot all the squirrels and rabbits you can eat," said Brad's father. "But leave deer hunting until I get back. If you did shoot a deer, most of the meat would spoil before you could eat it. And I don't want you to spend too much time traipsing through the woods after game."

"I suppose you don't want me to shoot a deer even if he threatens to attack me," Brad grumbled.

Mr. Porter smiled. "In all my born days I never heard of a deer attacking anybody," he said. "Now a moose is different. Better give a moose a wide berth if you see one. A moose can get a man down and kick him to death. A she-moose is one of the most dangerous animals on earth when she's protecting her young. But you're not likely to meet a moose if you keep pretty close to the cabin. Better not go far from the clearing. It's all too easy to get turned around and lost in the woods."

Brad ate his last spoonful of mush. He wished his father would stop telling him what to do and what not to do while he was up here alone.

Mr. Porter looked about the barren cabin and sighed. Except for a bunk against the wall and the bench he and Brad were sitting on there was no furniture. "I wish I could have made things more shipshape before I left," he said.

"I'll build another bench while you're gone." Brad was surprised to hear himself offering to do work he had not been told to do. "I'll see to everything," he said.

"I'll expect you to," said his father gravely, his serious blue eyes meeting Brad's gray ones. "Well, time for me to be on my way. Come help me get the canoe into the water."

On the way to the river, Brad stooped and picked a dogtooth violet. "Take it to Ma," he said.

"Be wilted long before I get to Boston. But give it here. I'll put it in my wallet. Maybe there'll be enough of it left for your mother to press between the leaves of her Bible."

The morning river gleamed like quicksilver. Small circular ripples showed where fish came to the surface to feed on insect eggs and flies.

"Wish I had remembered to pack the fishing tackle," said Brad. "Don't you forget to bring it, Pa."

26

"I won't," said Mr. Porter, with no reproach in his voice for Brad's forgetting.

He looked Brad straight in the eye, grasped his hand and gave it a firm shake. "Take care of yourself," he said.

Brad was impressed. His father had never shaken hands with him before. It made him feel almost grown up. "I'll make out all right," he said gruffly. "You don't need to worry about me."

Brad helped his father lift the boat into the water. Then he waded into the shallows and held the canoe steady while his father stepped in and sat down. It was hard for Brad to open his fingers and let go. He wanted to hold on to his father a minute longer.

Mr. Porter picked up his paddle. "Look for us in three weeks. Four at the outside. I'll get back as soon as I possibly can. Let go, Brad."

Brad gave the canoe a strong push out into the current and let go of it. He saw his father's paddle pick up the glistening water. The canoe moved away from him.

"Pa!" called Brad.

"What!"

"Don't forget the fishing tackle."

"I won't. Don't you forget to close the cabin door at night. Remember. Keep the door closed."

"I will. Good-by, Pa."

"Good-by."

"Good-by!" Brad shouted again through cupped hands. He watched until the canoe was out of sight around the bend in the river. Now he was the only living person up here in the woods. A wave of loneliness swept over him. The cawing of the crows sounded harsher than usual; the rustling of small animals in the underbrush seemed louder and more menacing.

"The animals outnumber me a thousand to one," he said aloud. "Maybe a million, if I count ants."

3

Alone

When Brad turned away from the river the cabin somehow looked smaller than it had a few minutes before. The clearing seemed only a pinprick in the vastness of the forest. A pine branch brushed against the cabin roof, as a gust of wind set the trees to murmuring mournfully. From the woods came a *tap, tap, tap,* like a blind man's cane. "A woodpecker," Brad reassured himself. He heard a whir, a feathery flutter of wings followed by a shrill squawk. There was cruelty in the woods.

"But there's nothing for me to be afraid of," Brad told himself. He remembered his promise to plant the corn and potatoes and went into the cabin for a spade. Soon, working in the sunlight, he lost his uneasiness.

29

It was easy to dig through the spongy layers of pine needles. Underneath them the ground was hard and there were many stones. Tree roots kept getting in the way of his spade. It was tiring work. Still, Brad kept at it until he had the earth spaded up between six stumps.

As he looked at the sun to see if it were nearly noon, Brad heard a bird sing one long, high note, followed by three quick low ones. Brad whistled the same notes and the bird answered. Pleased, Brad repeated the bird call. Even though he did not know what it meant, he liked being able to make the same sounds.

When he got back to the cabin, Brad found he was too tired to build the fire and cook a hot dinner. He poured plenty of molasses on the mush left over from breakfast and took the pewter porringer to a sunny ledge. When he had eaten, he stretched out on the wide rock. His eyes were on a level with a patch of wild strawberries just beginning to blossom. He would remember this patch. He watched an inchworm slowly climb a blade of grass. He saw an ant pulling a twig many times its size.

"Time to get at it again," his father would be saying if he were here. How far down river was he by now? Obeying his absent father, Brad got to work again.

Cutting up the seed potatoes, with two or three sprouts to each piece, was easier than digging. Brad laid aside four potatoes. His father had said he could eat that many.

He would eat two this week and two the next. They would be a real treat.

Planting the potatoes between the stumps was satisfying work. It was giving the Lord a hand in turning few into many. Brad hoped to have a fine crop of potatoes from these small pieces. He lugged water from the river for his garden. The plants would be well up and maybe in blossom by the time the family arrived.

It was too late in the day to put in the corn, Brad decided. That could wait till tomorrow. He started down the slope to the river to wash the dirt off his hands and bare feet. Ground hemlock stung his legs as he walked through the underbrush. When he had time, he would cut a path to the river.

The late afternoon sun made the river shadowy. It was almost colorless and so clear it mirrored the edges of the forest. Brad looked down river. How empty the river had seemed after his father had disappeared from view! Suddenly he heard a noise coming from upstream. He looked and saw four canoes coming rapidly toward him. Quickly he crouched behind the bushes. He peered out and saw that there were two Indian braves in each canoe. The strong strokes of their paddles sent the canoes swiftly past the spot where Brad hid. He scarcely had time to see their nearly naked bodies and their bronzed stern faces. He caught a few words of Indian language.

60768

Cody Memorial Library
Southwestern University
Georgetown, Texas

There was a wild, savage look about these men. Yet, crouching there watching them, Brad was aware that they, not he, were the native inhabitants of this Maine wilderness. Like the deer and other animals of the forest, they belonged here. For all he knew they might think these woods still were theirs. Then Brad remembered that his father had paid for his land. It was his.

"If they show any sign of coming ashore, I'll run to the cabin and get Pa's rifle," Brad told himself. He was so excited that the back of his neck prickled. "I'll be friendly if they are, but I'll let them see I have a gun. I'll defend the cabin with my last breath."

The sun flashed on the Indians' paddles. Not one of the canoes turned toward the shore. Soon they were out of sight.

"They couldn't see the cabin through the trees. They don't know anybody's here," Brad told himself, relieved. "I hope they don't catch up with Pa."

That night when Brad closed the cabin door he dragged the bench against it. He placed his father's rifle beside the bunk, close at hand if he needed it. He was not exactly scared, but he told himself that it paid to be on the safe side. The dark was lonely. Brad braced his spirits to meet it. "I'm getting along all right by myself," he thought. "But I'm glad the Indians don't know I'm here. I didn't put in a bad day's work today. Did as much as if Pa had been here to make me work. Wonder where he's sleeping tonight."

The next day was bright and fair. Brad's first waking thought was a desire for something filling to eat, for the day before had been slim picking. He got out the tinderbox and struck a fire and soon had salt-pork scraps frying and cornmeal mush cooking. "Have to eat to keep up my strength," he thought. "After breakfast I'll go out and shoot a rabbit and have a good rabbit stew for dinner. There'll be more salt pork left for the family if I shoot most of my meat."

Soon Brad was out in the woods near the clearing, his father's rifle in his hands, powder horn and pouch of bullets at his belt. "Don't be wasteful of powder and shot," he remembered his father had told him. Brad did not intend to be wasteful. He hoped he would bring down a rabbit with his first shot.

The shade of the woods was checkered with sunlight. A squirrel ran up a tree. Brad would not even aim at it today, with his mouth all set for rabbit. Should he shoot that chipmunk scampering over a rotten log? No, to eat chipmunk would be too much like eating mouse. That short-legged animal pattering toward him? A skunk. Whew, no! Skunk stew would taste awful. Here came a plump brown rabbit. As it stopped to nibble a leaf, Brad took careful aim, sighting along the barrel of the rifle.

He pressed the trigger and the noise of the shot pierced the quiet air. Brad saw the rabbit fall.

"I did get him my first shot," he boasted.

Brad was tempted to spend the rest of the day hunting in the woods. But he had promised not to shoot more game than he could eat. He had his dinner for today. He went back to the cabin and fanned the embers of the fire in the fireplace into a blaze. He put water on to boil while he skinned the rabbit. Then the meat went into the kettle to cook while Brad sat by the hearth and did nothing for a while. It seemed good not to be kept busy all the time. He had plenty of work to do but was in no hurry to start working. His father would not be back for weeks.

All Brad did the rest of the forenoon was to tend his stew and do a small job of whittling. He made pegs on which to hang his father's rifle beside the fireplace. He drove the sharply pointed pegs hard into the wall. By this time the rabbit was almost tender when Brad poked it with a fork. He cut one of his precious seed potatoes into his stew and thickened it slightly with cornmeal.

At last the stew was done. It tasted wonderful. Brad had grown tired of living on dried beans and fried salt-pork scraps while he and his father had been too busy to go hunting. It was no hardship to finish the rabbit in one meal, and the last mouthful tasted as good as the first.

"I'll have another rabbit tomorrow," he promised himself.

After a lazy hour of lying in the sunshine, Brad planted the corn. As he worked, he caught glimpses of the shining river beyond the trees. The water looked inviting. Brad decided to reward himself for planting the corn by having a good swim.

The water was so cold it set Brad's teeth to chattering. He had to swim fast to keep from getting numb. Because he wanted to be able to hide in a hurry if he saw any more Indian canoes coming down river, he kept close to the shore. But there were only shadows on the river. Nothing more.

"The Indians didn't find me yesterday. I'm not afraid they will," Brad told himself. "They must have all gone down river."

He amused himself for a few minutes after his swim, skipping stones in the river. Then he dressed and lugged a dozen round rocks for the chimney. He wished he knew how many rocks it would take to build the chimney. It would be a pity if he lugged too many. He began a pile of them beside the cabin.

Feeling thirsty, Brad went to the spring for a pail of water. The water bubbled up clear and cold, forming a small but deep pool fringed with tall grass. Brad had not been to the spring since the day before, and he saw that since then the grass on the far side of the pool had turned purple. Looking more closely, he saw that the bright sun had brought hundreds of violets into bloom.

"Wish Ma could see them," Brad thought. "Wish Prudy and Trudy were here to pick a bunch of violets for her. I'd make them pick long stems. Ma would be crazy about all these violets."

Brad dipped his pail in the spring. As he raised it, brimming with water, he noticed a large sheet of birch bark pinned to the trunk of the willow overlooking the spring. Where in the world had that come from? Who had pinned it there? Brad was so startled that he let go of the handle of the pail and let it sink in the spring as he ran to the tree.

The sheet of birch bark had been pinned to the trunk by a large thorn. Brad yanked it loose. "Indians!" he thought. "Indians have been here! Sometime last night or today they were this close to me."

Seeing Indians in canoes on the river had frightened Brad, but not half as much as realizing that they had been here on his father's land. Brad's hand was shaking as he held the bold, crude drawing on the sheet of birch bark. It was a picture of a bear in a canoe. Underneath the canoe was a line, and under that a circle. It was a message, Brad decided, but whether to him or to other Indians he could not tell.

Brad stared at the picture on the sheet of birch bark

Whoever had left the message might still be near, Brad thought. Even this minute Indians might have sneaked into the cabin. Some Indian brave might be taking the rifle from its pegs. The Indians might shoot him, scalp him. Horrid tales of Indian cruelty came to Brad's mind. Up here alone he would be at their mercy. They might burn the cabin. "No!" Brad cried aloud. "I won't let them do that. I won't."

He made himself walk back to the cabin. No smoke curled from its roof. It had not been set afire. He opened the cabin door inch by inch, his breath unsteady. He was scared, but he felt he had to do all he could to save the cabin. If Indians were in it and had not yet taken the rifle, he hoped he might dash in and grab it before they stopped him.

Now the door was wide enough to show him the empty cabin and his father's gun safe on its pegs. Brad let out his breath in a long sigh of relief. He felt weak now that his tenseness had left him. There was no sign that Indians had been in the cabin.

But Brad still had the birch-bark picture which proved that Indians had been at the spring. They might have landed from one of the canoes he had seen the afternoon before. Yet he had seen the canoes go by without landing. Perhaps another canoe had come by later and the Indians had come ashore to drink from the spring. Brad did not know. He wondered and worried, yet could not know.

Nor could Brad puzzle out the meaning of the picture of the bear in the canoe. He studied it more carefully. What did it mean? What could a picture of a bear in a canoe mean? He had no clue. He decided not to destroy the picture but to keep it. It would be something to show the family. With a sharp splinter of wood he tacked it to the wall.

"Probably the Indians were friendly Indians," he told himself. Yet when he went out to chop wood he took the rifle with him. He brought in a big stump, which he put in the fireplace. It would keep the fire burning all night long. As soon as it grew dark he would build a fire. "A fire's company," he said to himself, not acknowledging that tonight he might be glad to have a spot of light and warmth in the cabin.

Before going to bed, Brad again pulled the bench across the cabin door. "Pa needn't have worried that I wouldn't close the door nights," he thought. "Not with Indians roaming the woods. Wish I had a dog. He'd let me know if anybody was prowling outside." But Brad knew that with all the food supplies, tools, blankets, and cooking pots they had had to bring up river in the canoe, there had been no room for a dog.

He lay in his bunk and watched the firelight. He could

barely make out the birch-bark picture on the wall. "Guess I'll never know what that message means," he mused. "And I don't care. I hope I won't lay eyes on another Indian before Pa gets back."

Sleeping, he had a troubled dream of Indians chasing him. Their faces were bright with war paint and their tomahawks sharp and threatening. He woke up with a start and heard rain on the roof. He heard the wood sizzle as rain beating down the chimney hole put out the fire, leaving the cabin pitch dark.

"I never heard of Indians attacking in the rain," he comforted himself. He tried to stop thinking about Indians. He thought about the family instead, but that made him ache with loneliness. "But I'll get used to being alone," he told himself. "I have to. Anyway, I'd rather be alone than have Indians around. How could I tell if they were friendly? While I was trying to decide, they might capture me." Here he was thinking about Indians again. He turned his thoughts to going hunting in the woods. And soon he fell asleep and slept quite peacefully.

4

Lost

Two days later Brad began to keep a diary. As he had learned to do in school, he made a quill pen by splitting and sharpening the end of a long gray feather he had found in the woods. It pleased him to think he might be writing with a feather from an eagle's wing. For ink he mixed black soot with a little water. All the paper he could find was his father's chart, showing the location and extent of his land. If Brad made his entries brief, he would have plenty of space on the back of the chart to keep a record of all the days until the family arrived.

"*May 24,*" Brad wrote after his supper that day. "*Fair. Moderate winds. Shot squirrel. Ate squirrel. Lugged rocks for chimney. Watered garden.*"

Brad did not write that this was the day he had first seen ferns unfold in the woods. Or that he had held a cawing contest with the crows. He said nothing about how often he had thought of the family. He thought of the good bread his mother made; of his father's skill and exactness in building; of how the twins looked up at him, admiration in their blue eyes for their big brother.

Brad had never before done so much thinking and remembering. In his mind he revisited ships he had boarded in Boston harbor. If the embargo had not ruined the shipping trade, Brad might have gone to sea. His mother would have wanted to keep him at school, but his father would have realized that the sea could be a proper schoolmaster, Brad thought. Remembering the ever-changing ocean, Brad missed the tides. Up in the Maine woods close to the Penobscot River, he dreamed of the sea.

"May 25," Brad wrote by firelight. "Chilly. Rained most of the day. Cabin leaked some between logs. Made a three-legged stool for Prudy. Pork scraps, fried potatoes, and last of the salt codfish for dinner. A deer looked in the window."

It had been midmorning when Brad had looked up from his carpentry to see a deer poke his head through the opening cut in the logs that was the cabin's only window. The deer's eyes were deep brown and unafraid. Brad kept still so he would not startle him. Brad had not seen a living thing all morning and even a deer was company. He had no desire to shoot the animal. Brad was sorry when he withdrew his head and trotted off into the woods.

"May 26. More rain. Made three-legged stool for Trudy. Shot rabbit. Ate rabbit. Remembered to comb hair."

Brad put this last item in to please his mother, when she would read it. He remembered almost the last thing she had said to him when he had left Boston. "Don't get slack about your appearance while you're up in Maine by yourself. Remember you're up there to tame the wilderness, not to let it make you wild as a hawk. Do remember to comb your hair."

Brad recalled this advice from his mother and added another two words to his last entry of May 26. He did not want his mother to think that May 26 was the only day he had combed his hair. *"Remembered to comb hair as usual,"* the entry now read.

That was the night Brad was waked from a deep sleep by the howling of wolves outside. There was still glowing ash in the fireplace. Brad put on more wood and fanned it to a flame. Then he thought of the window hole. A wolf could leap through it. Brad sat on Prudy's stool with his father's rifle ready to aim at any dark head that might appear at the window. By the sound there were several animals outside. Yet none of them tried to get in

43

and after a while they went away. Then Brad went back to bed and slept until the sun was high and the wet woods glistened in sunlight. He made no mention of his terror by night in his diary the next day, partly because he had all but forgotten it.

"May 27," he wrote the next evening. *"Stepped in hornet's nest. Got stung. Went for swim in afternoon."*

That morning Brad had been watching the flight of an eagle and had not looked where he was stepping. His bare foot had come down on the hornet's nest. He left that place in a hurry. He plastered his fourteen stings with river mud, but the pain and the poison from them made him slightly feverish. That day, though he spent some time daubing moist clay in the chinks between the logs of the cabin, he did not accomplish much. He found the cool river soothing to his hurts. Before, he had swum in the shallows. This afternoon he had let himself float until he was in the full strength of the current. The river had almost been too strong for him, and he had had to fight to get back to shore. He could have written *"nearly drowned,"* in his diary.

"May 28. Morning fair and warmer. Hailstorm in afternoon. Had fried rabbit and ice water for supper."

It had been about three in the afternoon, Brad judged, when such a black cloud was overhead that it seemed like twilight. Brad was outside the cabin, looking up at

44

the sky, when hail pelted down, stinging like pebbles. He ran inside and watched the hail fall past the window hole. A few of the pellets fell inside. Brad picked one up. "Big as a pullet's egg!" he marveled, wishing he could keep one to show the family, for they would never believe a hailstone could be that big. He scooped up enough to make all the ice water he could drink. He could have frozen ice cream with them if he had had the cream.

May 29 was clear but cold. It seemed like a throwback to March. The next day warmed up around noon. Brad faithfully recorded the weather every day in his diary, for his life was greatly influenced by its changes. Cool crisp mornings made him feel like getting at some of the chores his father had told him to do. The stack of firewood behind the cabin grew on cool days. The pile of stones for the fireplace became higher more slowly, for Brad brought stones for the fireplace only on his way back from swimming, and then usually but two at a time.

Rainy days made getting meals a hardship, for rain coming down the chimney hole either made the fire smoke or put it out. During a hard storm Brad often ate cold food rather than struggle to keep the fire burning. When there were three rainy days in a row, Brad spent many hours working on another bench for the cabin. He was careful not to use many nails, for handmade nails were expensive and he knew his father used them sparingly. The first two days of stormy weather, Brad kept pretty much to the cabin, but by the third day he was out in the dripping woods. His clothes felt clammy anyway. It was not much change to get wet to the skin. The forest smelled dank. It seemed empty of all life, for the birds and the animals had sought shelter from the rain. Brad had never felt more alone.

Bright days made him forget rainy ones. In the sunshine he spent an entire morning watching beavers build a dam across a stream. Another day he found a den of foxes. He wanted to take one of the baby foxes for a pet but he was afraid it was too young to live away from its mother. The little foxes were of a lighter red-brown than their mother. The back of their ears was marked with black. They looked something like puppies except for their bushy tails.

For more than a week after he had found the birch-bark picture at the spring, Brad took his father's rifle with him every time he left the cabin. But as time passed and he saw no further sign of Indians, his fear of them grew less. He stopped thinking he saw Indians lurking behind trees at dusk, and no longer did nightmares about Indians wake him in the night, sweating from fright. His dread of Indians was pushed to the back of his mind, and he took the rifle with him only when he went hunting. Now and then the picture of the bear in the canoe

46

reminded him of Indians, yet after a while he grew so used to it that he hardly saw it.

Brad's father had started down river the twenty-first of May. Brad figured that the earliest he could get back would be the eleventh of June. It might be a week later, but Brad intended to have everything ready by the earliest date. Most of the week before the tenth he kept busy. He chopped wood until the woodpile was nearly as high as his head. He walled the spring. He lugged more stones for the fireplace. He finished chinking the cabin walls. His burst of industry made up for the days when he had not exerted himself. He had everything done by the ninth of June, two days before the family could possibly arrive.

The morning of the tenth found Brad with time on his hands. He could not spend the day just waiting for the next one. He decided to work at an extra task that would please his mother. He would make her a wild-flower garden. He spaded up a small plot of ground on the sunniest side of the cabin. When that was done he went into the woods to search for wild flowers to transplant, taking the rifle along in case a rabbit crossed his path. If he made rabbit stew today it might keep until the family arrived.

Gun over shoulder and open jackknife in hand, Brad first wandered about in the woods near the clearing. He dug up a few clumps of perky white bunchberry flowers, some star flowers, and two lady's-slippers. Golden sunshine filtered through the branches of the pines. It was a lovely day. He might find prettier flowers deeper in the forest, he thought. He would be in no danger of getting lost, he assured himself, if he blazed the trunks of the trees as he went. With his jackknife he peeled off pieces of bark shoulder height. He made his blaze marks at frequent intervals so he would have no difficulty finding his way back to the clearing.

He soon came to a spot of deep shade. There were great growths of fungus under the trees or attached to the trunks. One, dark brown and shiny on one side, had an underside as white as the belly of a fish. The trees were crowded so close that a dead tree stood propped up by its neighbors. Brad saw sow bugs and ants busy in its rotten wood.

Brad pushed through to woods less dense. He found high mounds of ferns formed by many generations of dead ferns, with new growth on top making a bright green covering. He stepped on one of the mounds and his legs sank in up to his knees. Ferns like these grew near the cabin. He did not want any of them for his mother's garden, but he stopped under a hemlock to dig up a dainty maidenhair fern. He knew his mother would like that.

He smelled pink twinflowers growing up a mossy slope. He was careful to get roots and all when he dug several vines of them. And his mother would be sure to want some of the goldthread flowers. He had heard her say that their delicate gold-colored stems were good for the tooth-ache. A jack-in-the-pulpit plant went into his trouser pocket to join other flowers. If he kept on he would be a walking flower garden!

He went deeper into the woods. He broke through thick underbrush and there, to his surprise, was a shim-mering sea of grass, a natural meadow. Not far from him a deer and her fawn were cropping grass. They paid no attention to him. They had not caught his scent. Brad had no impulse to shoot them. They were so beautiful and so much a part of the landscape that he did not need to remember that his father had told him not to shoot a deer.

Wild strawberries grew in the grass. Brad picked clusters of ripe berries big as thimbles. They were juicy and sweet, the first fruit of the season. Nothing, Brad thought, could taste or smell better than sun-warmed wild strawberries.

Brad was so busy picking and eating strawberries that he did not notice when other animals beside the deer came into the meadow. He suddenly looked up and saw a cow moose and her calf. They were close enough for

49

Brad to see the powerful shoulders and broad chest of the cow moose. She looked like a deer, he thought, but much larger and stronger and with no look of deerlike softness in her eyes. He caught a look of anger and hate as the big animal rushed toward him with a snort of rage.

There was no time to raise his gun and shoot. Brad's only hope lay in the speed of his legs. He ran and the moose ran after him. And Brad, remembering his father's warning about a moose, knew he was running for his life.

Half around the meadow they went, with Brad barely keeping ahead. A pain grew in his side. His legs ached and his breath came in shuddering gasps even after he got his second wind. It was torture to go on but he must. To slow down would mean death. He had to keep running.

Brad left the meadow and ran into the woods, thinking he would be able to dodge the moose better there. He forgot that the moose was more at home in the woods than he was. Branches slapped Brad as he pushed through them. Briars scratched him. He did not feel the pain. Not while just behind him he heard branches snap like twigs at the thrust of the powerful body of the moose. She was almost up with him. In another minute she would be at him with her punishing hoofs. Brad knew he could run no faster. He could not get away; he was a goner.

Brad stayed up the tree until the moose went away

In his desperate haste, he bumped into a tree. More instinct than conscious thought sent him climbing up into the branches. The moose saw him climb the tree. She pushed against the trunk till it swayed, but Brad hung on. Angrily the moose snorted and pawed the ground. Brad saw the dark brown hide ripple over the powerful muscles. She was as big or bigger than an ox. She could have killed him easily. It seemed a long time before she gave up getting him out of the tree and galloped away.

Brad stayed in the tree until he was sure she had gone for good. Not until he was on the ground again did he realize that he had lost his father's rifle. Somewhere along the way in his frenzied run, he had dropped it. He must find it. For what would he do without a rifle? What would his father say when he learned it was lost? But it must not stay lost. Brad determined to find it. He searched and searched. He tried to retrace his steps, and could not even find the meadow again. He did not find the rifle. Nor could he find the trees he had blazed to show him the way back to the clearing. With sinking heart, Brad realized that he had not only lost his father's rifle but himself.

"Now don't get panicky," Brad told himself sternly. Yet only chance, he knew, would lead him back the way he had come. He had completely lost all sense of direction, but he kept walking.

By the sun overhead Brad knew it was noon. Then long past noon. He climbed ledges, broke through underbrush, and scaled a giant boulder, hoping to see the meadow or the river — anything that would show him the way back to the clearing. All he saw were miles and miles of unbroken forest.

"If I could break out to the river, I'd be all right," Brad thought. But which way was the river? He might be going in the opposite direction.

When late afternoon came, Brad was still walking. He had tripped on roots and fallen down twice, the last time cutting his knee on a stone. A trickle of blood had run down his leg and dried. As the afternoon shadows deepened, Brad thought of the wild animals in the forest: the wildcats, the wolves, the bears. Cruel eyes might be watching him now, waiting for the darkness before attacking him.

He came to a giant pine that towered above all its neighbors. It was taller even than the big tree that had so nearly crushed him when he and his father had been cutting down trees before building the cabin. There was soft moss under the tall pine. Brad flung himself down on it. He was exhausted. Exhausted and discouraged.

Suddenly a hopeful thought came to him. From the top of this towering tree he might be able to see the river, the silver thread that would lead him back to the cabin.

"Why didn't I think of that before?" he asked himself. "I'll be at the top of this tree in two shakes of a lamb's tail."

He clasped the trunk as far up as he could reach and tried to climb. The massive trunk was slippery with balsam. It was like climbing a greased pole. The lowest branches of the pine were far above his head. He had nothing to cling to. He slipped and fell — tried again and again and still slipped and fell. His legs and arms were sore and his hands and clothes black with pitch before Brad gave up trying to climb the pine. He stood under it and all but wept.

Off in the distance he heard a sound that was half bark, half cough. He drew out his knife, a small weapon against the wild animals of the forest. He brushed dirt from the knife blade. Most of the flowers he had so carefully dug had fallen out of his pockets while he had been running from the moose. A few wilted twinflowers trailed from one pocket. He did not throw them away, though he thought it doubtful if his mother ever would have her flower garden. How long ago the morning seemed!

A large pine cone fell from the tree. On the way to the ground it rested briefly on the branch of a small fir that grew close to the pine. Brad saw the falling cone. It gave him an idea. If he cut a small tree and propped it against the big pine, he might be able to climb the small tree

54

until he reached the lowest branch of the pine. Then, with branches to help him, he could climb to the top.

"It's worth trying," he told himself.

Quickly he set to work to cut down a fir sapling with his jackknife. If fir had not been soft wood, Brad could not have cut it. Once the blade of his knife bent. He caught his breath. If it broke, he thought that his last slim hope would be gone. The shadows were deep and the forest almost in darkness before he had cut a ring an inch deep around the base of the fir. He grasped the trunk and leaned all his weight against it. And lost his balance and fell to the ground with it when the trunk snapped.

He propped the fir against the pine. The top of the fir was touching the big tree, and the base slanted slightly outward. Brad wedged the base with stones. He hoped and prayed that the slender tree would bear his weight.

Up he went. He was near the top of the fir when the wood cracked. First the part leaning against the pine, and then the whole tree, fell. But Brad had had time to grasp the lowest branch of the pine. He swung in mid-air for an instant, then managed to pull himself up. He was safe on a stout branch. Brad had climbed the masts of ships. Now the branches were like stays to help him up. He was soon at the top of the giant pine.

He looked down on a sea of trees. Then, blessedly close, he saw the river. He almost cried with relief. He memorized the landmarks that led to it. The stump of the fir he had cut was like an arrow pointing the way. Beyond the fir was a long ledge and then a last barrier of trees between the ledge and the river.

In the gathering dusk, Brad walked toward the ledge. For an awful moment he could not find it and was afraid he had lost his way again. He climbed a boulder and saw the ledge was near. He could catch a glimpse of the river beyond the trees.

Brad came to the river while the afterglow was still in the sky. He was near the bend. The clearing was just beyond. In a few minutes he would be back to the cabin.

Thankful though he was to have found his way home, Brad felt very much alone as he entered the cabin. There was nobody there to hear about his adventures in the woods. He would even have been glad to be scolded. The trees stood dark and tall around the small clearing. "We almost had you this time," sang the wind in the pines.

"Thank goodness the family will get here tomorrow or next day," he told himself. "I'm tired of living by myself."

Brad wished his mother had been there to get him some supper. He was too tired to do anything but flop down on his bunk to rest. "I'll get up in a little while and get something to eat," he thought, remembering he had not eaten since morning. "But I just have to rest first."

The cabin was hot. The sun had been on its roof all

day. Brad left the cabin door open to cool the room off. "I'll close it when I get up to get my supper," he thought.

A rising wind set branches to brushing against the cabin roof. To Brad they sounded like claws trying to scratch through.

"The forest really is an enemy," he thought. "It doesn't want me here."

Brad fell asleep almost as soon as he had stretched out on the bunk. Nor did he wake up to get his supper and to close the cabin door. He slept until broad daylight and might have gone on sleeping even longer if a strange noise in the cabin had not waked him.

5

Waiting

Brad sat up. Still drowsy, he could hardly believe his eyes. For an instant he thought he was dreaming that the bear in the birch-bark picture had stepped out of its canoe and was on all fours in front of the fireplace. Then Brad came wide awake. A real bear was in the cabin with him. A big black bear was making guttural noises as it rooted about, its nose to the cabin floor. The bear must have been there some time. It had helped itself to all the food supplies in the cabin.

With horror Brad saw that the bear had clawed open the sack of cornmeal. It had tipped over the crock of salt pork. Brine from the salt pork was mingled with molasses from the overturned molasses jug. All that was left of the salt pork was gnawed rinds. Everything the bear had not eaten it had spilled and fouled.

Hearing Brad move, the bear raised its head, its muzzle caked with cornmeal and dripping with molasses. Then it went to licking up molasses again. The bear showed no sign of being afraid of Brad.

Brad was so angry he forgot to be afraid. "You dirty thief!" he shouted. "You pig of a bear! You — " Words failed him. He rushed to the fireplace and picked up the heavy cast-iron frying pan. "Get out of here," he bawled, whacking the bear on the rump. "Get out!"

The bear was too full of food to be quarrelsome. The big beast ambled awkwardly to the open cabin door. It walked away, leaving a mess on the cabin floor that was a dreadful sight to behold.

It took Brad a long time to get the cabin decent again. There was nothing left that was fit to eat. Except for some leftover cornmeal mush in the big kettle, Brad was entirely without food. Nor could he get meat, now that he had lost his father's rifle. Instead of having a good supply of food when the family arrived, he would have nothing.

"Lucky for me they'll be along sometime today or tomorrow," Brad told himself. To be sure, his father had said it might be four weeks before he was back, yet he would try to make it in three. It was three weeks to the day today, and Brad expected the family. It would not be like his father to make a slow journey. "Even if they don't come till tomorrow I won't get very hungry," Brad thought, remembering the patch of wild strawberries near the river.

Brad would have looked forward to the family's arrival more happily if there had not been the matter of the lost gun and the open cabin door to explain. If he had not gone so far from the clearing, he might not have lost the rifle. If he had not fallen asleep, leaving the cabin door open, the bear would not have gotten in.

He tried to excuse himself. He had thought that by blazing his trail he could not get lost in the forest. It had not been his fault that the cow moose had attacked him. Nor was the open cabin door much his fault. He had not meant to leave it open all night. As Brad swept dirty cornmeal onto a piece of bark with a brush broom he suddenly remembered something his father had said to him. "Nature doesn't forgive carelessness or forgetfulness."

In Boston it was no sin to get lost. A person asked his way of any stranger. Nor was an open door a crime. It did not seem fair to Brad that life was harsher up here in the Maine woods. That meaning well did not count. He thought he had been punished too severely. He dreaded to tell his father what had happened.

Brad decided that he could not expect the family until late afternoon. Until they came he would work hard doing little extra things that would please them. Then they might not blame him so much for the lost gun and the spoiled food.

He made a path to the spring, trimming off the overhanging branches of trees and placing flat stones in damp hollows. He went with his jackknife from spruce tree to spruce tree, digging out chunks of spruce gum for the twins. From near the spring he dug up clumps of violets and daisies for his mother's wild-flower garden. They were not rare, like the flowers he had lost the day before, but he transplanted and watered them with great care. They drooped in the sun. Transplanting was hard both for flowers and people, Brad reflected.

"It won't really seem like home to me up here till the family comes," he told himself. Now that the time of their arrival was near, he could hardly bear to wait.

In the afternoon Brad went out to the river to watch for his father's canoe. The river was empty. Under a sky that had turned cloudy since noon, the water looked more like space than substance. There was a lonely look about it.

Brad could not see far down river from where he stood. In order to see beyond the bend he walked downstream to the high ledge that overlooked the river. He clambered up the steep slope at the back. From the top he looked down on the birch grove that fringed the river below the ledge. The trunks of the birches were far enough apart to give Brad a clear view down river. His eyes yearned for the sight of his father's canoe rounding the bend.

Brad sat watching the river until dusk. The family had not come. "But they'll be sure to get here tomorrow," Brad told himself as he went back to the cabin. He had finished the cornmeal mush at noon. There was not a thing in the house to eat. He went to bed hungry.

Brad's family did not come the next day, or the next. Or still the next. Each night Brad thought they would surely come the next day. His eyes ached from looking in vain. The river was always empty.

By the end of a week of living on berries and water, Brad was little more than skin and bones. Slight by nature, his skin and his eyes now seemed too big for the rest of him. There were never nearly enough berries to satisfy his hunger. The wild strawberry crop was almost gone and the blueberries were still green. Brad chewed a handful of the small, hard berries; they made him sick. A few early raspberries were only a tantalizing taste in his mouth.

All one afternoon Brad tried to catch a fish in his hands. He waded into the river and stood perfectly still, his hands ready. Once a fish touched his hand but he could not move fast enough to grasp it. He went back to the cabin and unraveled yarn from the end of a blanket. He whittled a hook from wood and cut a fishpole. Now he had line, pole, and hook, and he tied a small stone to the line for a sinker. He baited his wooden hook with a worm and swung it into the water. He felt a nibble, then a bite. He gave a jerk to set the hook and then quickly raised his line. He had caught a fish. But the yarn line broke before he had raised the fish more than a few inches from the water. He was sick with disappointment. If only he had remembered to bring the fishing tackle to Maine he would not be starving. The punishment for that moment of forgetfulness seemed cruelly heavy.

He threw his useless fish pole on the ground and went to hunt for berries. Thoughts of good food plagued him. Daisies in the grass reminded him of beautiful fried eggs. He thought of a crisp slice of ham to go with the eggs. He remembered how good his mother's dried apple pies tasted — he could eat a whole one. He dreamed of golden-brown baked beans and thick slices of steamed brown bread. He imagined hot cream-of-tartar biscuit dripping with butter, crisp doughnuts hot out of the fat, golden custard with meringue on top, rich spice cake. Dreams of food did not fill the aching emptiness in his stomach. Even to think of food was aggravating, yet he could not keep his thoughts away from it.

It was now past the latest time Mr. Porter had told Brad to expect him. He had been gone over a month, yet Brad went on looking for him. The ledge overlooking the river was his watchtower. Every day he spent hours gazing down river, watching for a canoe that did not come.

The first few days of his waiting, Brad had taken pains to keep himself tidy, his face and hands clean, his hair combed. As he grew weak with hunger, he no longer cared how he looked. It seemed too much effort even to comb his hair. All that mattered was to keep alive until the family came. How long, he wondered, could a person live without eating? But of course the family would be here before he starved to death.

Two weeks after the bear had destroyed all his food, Brad woke up, after a troubled night's sleep, and heard rain on the cabin roof. It was weeping weather and Brad wept, too. Lying in his bunk, listening to the falling rain, Brad finally gave up hope of his family's coming. They must be dead. Perhaps their canoe had capsized and they had drowned. Or they might have been ambushed by Indians. Brad's fear of Indians had revived after he had lost his father's rifle and no longer had a weapon to use against them. The thought of savage Indians scalping his little twin sisters made Brad shiver, yet the image seemed horribly real.

A feeling of sadness overwhelmed him. "Pa and Ma

and the twins are dead, and I'm up here alone starving to death," he moaned.

Brad thought of his father — of his strength and firmness of character. Brad was sure that if his father had been killed it had not been without fighting bravely.

"Pa would expect me to do the same," Brad said aloud.

But what could he do? "I'll walk down river," Brad decided. "I'll keep on walking just as long as I hold out."

It was almost fifty miles down river to Old Town. Farther than that to Bangor, the first white settlement. A strong man might fight his way through the dense woods along the river, though at times it might take him an hour to go half a mile. Brad was so weak that, with no food to eat along the way except berries, it would be a miracle if he got halfway. He knew this, yet he decided to set out.

"If I hadn't waited so long for them I would have more of a chance," Brad thought, "but anyway I'm going. Pa wouldn't think much of me if I just sat still and starved to death."

The rain was wet on Brad's face when he went to the spring for a last drink of water. After this he would be drinking from the river. Leaning over the spring, he felt so dizzy he nearly fell in. "Steady," he told himself.

Now he was closing the cabin door. He felt sad to leave so much of the work of his hands: the clearing he had helped chop from the forest, the cabin he had partly built, the woodpile — so many hours of labor! — his mother's small flower garden, the stools he had made with such care for his little sisters. Near the door he picked up a strong stick to use for a cane, for his steps were unsteady.

As he walked away from the cabin, the rain stopped yet the trees went on weeping. It was a gentle morning with no wind. The sky was soft gray, the river silvery.

He came out to the river just above the cliff where he had spent so many hours watching the river. Habit made him start up the steep slope again. He had no hope that he would see the long-expected canoe. Yet he felt he must look one more time down the stretch of river.

He fell once, getting up the slope of the cliff, and had to cling to bushes or he would have fallen several more times. Once at the top, he had to sit down and rest for a moment. Then he got to his feet and, with the help of his cane, walked toward the edge of the cliff. From here he could get the best view of the river. It gleamed like mother-of-pearl as the sun burned through the clouds and mist. As it had been so many times before, the river was empty.

Everything was very still. The river moved silently. No birds sang. There was no murmur of pines in the wind-less air.

Suddenly Brad heard a noise. It was coming from the birch grove below the cliff where he stood. He looked

down and saw two Indians stripping birch bark from a tree. The bark came off in a big curving arc.

Brad stood stock-still. He could not have moved if he had tried. He saw the glistening bodies naked to the waist, the long knives, the dark, savage faces. It was as if he saw his fear become alive. Here were the Indians he had so long dreaded to see. Weak as he was, with no rifle to protect him, he would be helpless if they attacked him.

"I must get away before they see me," Brad thought. But he seemed unable to move. His muscles were locked with fear.

The Indians looked fierce and strong. One of them was a man taller than Brad's father. The other was a boy about Brad's height but heavier built and broader-shouldered.

Suddenly the Indian boy looked up and caught sight of Brad standing at the edge of the ledge. The young Indian pointed at him and spoke to the older Indian. Now both Indians called out to him. Then, with their long knives in their hands, they started toward him.

"They're coming after me," Brad thought. "Don't scalp me!" he felt like screaming, but kept silent. No matter what the Indians did to him, he must not show fear.

Brad found he was able to move again. He took one quick step backward and slipped on a loose stone; tried to keep his balance and failed. He fell headlong down the steep side of the cliff. He felt himself falling and then felt nothing more as he landed hard and lay unconscious at the feet of the two Indians.

6

The Bear in the Canoe

When Brad came back to consciousness, he was lying on his bunk in the cabin. His head ached. He put up his hand and felt a bump on his forehead as big as a hen's egg. But the worst pain was in his right ankle. When he moved it, the pain was so sharp that he moaned. Immediately the Indian boy Brad had seen from the cliff came over to him. The sharp knife was still in his hand. Brad was afraid that the Indian had been waiting for him to come to consciousness before scalping him. He tried to sit up. The Indian boy gently but firmly pushed him down. Brad was too weak to resist. He noticed that the Indian boy smelled of ozone, sweat, and rancid grease. Since he had not made any threatening movement with

69

the knife, Brad decided that the boy might not be un-friendly. Yet it was too soon to tell.

When Brad made no further effort to sit up, the young Indian went over and squatted down in front of the fire-place. Brad saw that he was cutting meat into the iron kettle which had been empty for so long. He had built a fire, and the flickering flames lit up his bronzed skin, his high cheek bones. He wore a red feather in his headband. He could mean no harm if he were cooking food, Brad decided, and fell into a troubled sleep.

Brad waked as the Indian boy raised him up and held a cup of soup to his lips. It was hot and strong. Brad drank it gratefully. Instead of scalping him, the Indian boy was feeding him.

The taller, older Indian was not in sight. The two boys were alone in the cabin.

"Did you bring me here?" Brad asked, in a voice so weak it did not seem his own.

The Indian boy shook his head to show that he did not understand. He went to the wall and took down the birch-bark picture. Bringing it over to Brad, he pointed first to himself and then to the bear in the canoe. How this could make sense Brad could not see. The Indian boy put his finger on the line and the circle under the bear. He pointed upward, tracing a circle with a pointed finger. He spoke words Brad could not understand. Now Brad

shook his head. He was sure of this much, however —
this Indian boy was the one who had pinned the birch-
bark picture to the tree near the spring. How many times
had he been near the cabin? How did it happen that the
boy had come today, just in time to save him from starving, Brad wondered. He was too weak to care much right
now, yet he felt grateful.

He watched the Indian boy squat by the kettle on the
hearth, reach in, and bring out a dripping piece of meat,
which he ate in his fingers.

"Give me some," Brad begged. He sat up and made
motions to show that he, too, wanted some of the meat.

The Indian boy shook his head. Apparently soup was
all Brad was going to get at this time. He lay back and
dozed. When he opened his eyes, it was growing dark
in the cabin, and he was alone.

Had the Indian boy abandoned him? Brad knew that
with his hurt ankle he might not even be able to drag
himself to the spring for water. He could not possibly
walk down river. He could not even start. He would die
up here alone. Brad moved painfully to the edge of the
bunk. He tried to stand. Pain stabbed his ankle. His head
swam. He fainted and fell.

Brad was not unconscious long. He heard the cabin
door open and saw the Indian boy come in, a dead rabbit
dangling from one hand. He helped Brad back on the

bunk and scolded him in Indian language. Then he gave him another cup of soup, this time with shreds of meat in it. Brad knew he should eat slowly, since his stomach was so unaccustomed to solid food, but he could not help cramming the meat in his mouth.

"Good!" Brad said. "Good!" He thought the Indian boy understood that word. He did not smile, yet Brad sensed he liked having his food appreciated.

Pain and his long fast made Brad feverish. As in a dream he watched the Indian boy skin the rabbit, throw the skin into a corner, and cut the meat into the kettle. He separated the logs, so the fire would burn more slowly. "What will he do next?" Brad wondered.

He was not long in doubt. The Indian boy walked over to the bunk and motioned for Brad to move against the wall. When Brad had painfully moved over, the Indian lay down beside him. Brad did not mind his smell. Brad knew now without a doubt that the Indian boy was friendly, for one does not lie down to sleep in the same bed with an enemy.

The Indian boy went to sleep almost at once. Brad lay awake. It was warm in the cabin, though the door was open. Apparently the Indian feared no visit from bears. Brad's fever made him restless. If he moved, the pain in his ankle grew sharper. He tried to lie still, though he wanted to toss and turn.

How strange it was to have been befriended by an Indian! "Even Pa would be surprised," Brad thought. A surge of grief for his family brought tears to his eyes. Not knowing what had happened to them made his sorrow even worse. The pain of grief blended with the ache of his ankle. He hurt all over. Yet something within him was, in spite of everything, glad to be alive.

At last Brad slept fitfully. When he woke it was broad daylight. The cabin was full of the delicious smell of stewing meat. The Indian boy was not in the cabin, but this time Brad was pretty sure he would be back. In a few minutes he came in, soft-footed in his moccasins. He held birch bark rolled into a horn shape and filled with red raspberries.

"They must have ripened in the night. I could find only a few yesterday," Brad thought.

Brad sat up, though it made him dizzy. He watched the Indian boy bring the kettle to the bunk and squat down beside it. The Indian boy reached in the kettle for a piece of meat and motioned for Brad to do the same. Brad reached his thin hand in, slightly burning his fingers as he brought out a bone with plenty of meat on it. Brad bit into it. My, it tasted good!

When his hunger was satisfied, the Indian wiped his greasy fingers on his deerskin breechcloth and tried to talk to Brad.

73

"Sabattis," he said, pointing to his chest.

He was telling his name, Brad realized. So Brad pointed to himself. "Brad," he said. "Brad."

The Indian boy repeated the name, which sounded strange as he said it. He spoke several sentences, but Brad had no idea what they meant and he was too weak to make much effort to understand. In spite of the Indian boy's kindness to him, Brad missed his mother's care. She had always been so good to him when he was ill! He tried to stop thinking of her, yet the ache of loss was so sharp that he hardly noticed when the Indian boy left.

Sabattis was not gone long. He brought back a tiny bird bone and threadlike roots. He swiftly knotted the roots to form a line. He was getting ready to go fishing, Brad realized. "Why didn't I think of using a bone for a hook and roots for line?" Brad asked himself. When his fishing tackle was ready, Sabattis went outdoors, and Brad was alone again with his grief and his pain.

In midmorning the cabin door opened, and the tall, older Indian stood in the doorway. He came in as silently as light. He carried a deerskin gathered into a sack over his shoulder, and his right hand held a bow. A quiver of arrows hung from a belt richly embroidered in purple and white shells. A necklace of bear claws rested on his chest. His face was strong-featured, as if hewn from brownstone. His black eyes were piercing and proud.

74

"Me Chief Kineowa," he said. "Sabattis, my son. Friend, white boy."

"I guess you Indians saved my life. I'm much obliged to you," said Brad earnestly.

"No understand. No speak much English," said Chief Kineowa. He put down the deerskin sack, and as it fell open Brad could see it contained many ears of dried corn. When he had propped his bow against the wall, the chief came over to Brad. He probed his ankle with strong fingers.

Brad had to grit his teeth not to cry out. He had heard that Indians did not flinch when they felt pain, and he wanted to show that a white boy could be just as brave.

Chief Kineowa stopped hurting him. "Good," he said. Brad guessed that he might mean that the ankle was sprained but not broken.

The chief opened a small deerskin pouch at his waist and brought out a big gob of grease. He smoothed this thickly over Brad's ankle. "No walk," he said, and held up all ten fingers.

Brad hoped the chief meant ten days and not ten weeks. He watched the Indian take the blanket from the bunk and tear off a narrow strip as easily as if the strongly woven wool had been paper. Brad tried not to wince as the Indian bound his ankle tightly with the strip of blanket.

Chief Kineowa's eye fell on the birch-bark picture, which Sabattis had pinned back on the wall. "I tell you," he said, and took the picture down and brought it to Brad's bunk. Then the chief whittled a sharp stick and rubbed the end of it thick with soot from the fireplace. He came over to the bunk, picked up the sheet of birch bark, and put it face down on the floor. Squatting in front of it, he began to draw. Brad watched him draw four circles and a line beneath them.

"Me go four moons," the chief said quite plainly.

Did he mean that he and Sabattis were leaving him alone for four months? Brad wondered in alarm. Even if the Indian left the dried corn, Brad felt that he could not possibly live that long by himself. How could he manage before he could walk?

"Don't leave me alone," he begged.

Just then the cabin door opened and Sabattis came in. A large fish dangled from his hand. Unsmilingly he greeted his father in Indian language. He showed the fish, trying to hide his pride in his catch.

Chief Kineowa gave a grunt which seemed to signify approval of the fish. He picked up the sheet of birch bark and held it in front of Brad. This time he was showing Brad the side on which was drawn the picture of the bear in the canoe.

"*Awesus*," the chief said several times, pointing first to

Chief Kineowa explained the birch-bark picture to Brad

himself and Sabattis and then to the bear.

Brad could not make out what the chief meant. Then suddenly Brad remembered that tribes of Indians often took the names of animals. It was quite likely that both Sabattis and his father had tried to tell him that they belonged to the bear family. Brad had understood when the chief had told him that a circle meant a moon. Why, this was what the bear in the canoe picture must mean: The Indians had landed from a canoe one moon ago. They had left a message saying they would return in one moon. That was it. Now Brad felt he understood the picture of the bear in the canoe. But he dreaded the thought that the message on the back of the birch bark meant that the Indians were now leaving him for four months. Brad's thin face showed his worry.

Chief Kineowa stood tall and straight. He put a hand on Sabattis' shoulder. "He stay. I go," he said. "You brothers. I come back four moons." Then he and Sabbatis talked together earnestly in Indian language. Sabattis scowled. He did not seem to be liking what his father was saying to him.

Brad was sorry to see the tall chief go. With no word of farewell or backward glance, he stalked to the door. Some of the sunlight in the cabin seemed to go out with him.

So Brad was left alone with the Indian boy, Sabattis.

Brad sensed that the Indian boy was not too well pleased to be left to take care of him. Sabattis continued to scowl all the time he was cleaning the fish. He still looked sullen as he hung the kettle half-full of water over the fire. He flung a handful of wood ashes in the kettle and then shelled a few ears of dried corn. When the water was boiling, he put in the corn. Brad had seen his mother make hulled corn the same way.

Soon the boys were sharing a dinner of fried fish and hulled corn. By this time Sabattis looked in a better humor. When Brad pointed at the corn and said, "Hulled corn," Sabattis made a try at repeating the English words.

"*Skamuni*," Sabattis then said to Brad, giving the corn its name in Penobscot Indian. "*Kineo*," he said, showing Brad a stone.

The word for stone and the name of Sabattis' father were much alike, Brad thought. And that seemed fitting, for there was something about Chief Kineowa that was like rock, strong and enduring.

"Kettle," said Brad, pointing to the cast-iron cooking pot.

But Sabattis had tired of learning English words. He went outside and soon returned with a thin flat slab of rock and a chunky small one. He put these on Brad's bunk and hauled over the sack of corn to where Brad could reach it. Brad understood from Sabattis' gestures that he

79

was to shell corn and grind it into cornmeal.

Brad thought he caught a hint of contempt in the Indian boy's face as he set Brad to doing squaw work. But he was in no position to object.

Sabattis took up his fishing tackle and went out again. He was taking care of Brad, but that did not include staying in with him all the time.

Brad did not really mind. He was still very weak. When he had shelled three ears of corn and had pounded the kernels into coarse meal, he went to sleep. He felt stronger when he woke up. What had wakened him was Sabattis coming in with three good-sized trout.

"He's a good fisherman, but so am I," Brad thought. He hoped he would soon be well enough to show that he, too, could catch fish.

Sabattis said a string of words in Indian. He seemed to be scolding Brad for not having pounded more corn into cornmeal. At least you should be able to do squaw work, Sabattis' attitude said.

Brad could tell that the Indian boy thought him stupid because he did not speak Indian; weak and inferior because he had not known how to get along by himself in the woods during that time when he had nearly starved. Probably Sabattis thought him a careless fool to have fallen down the cliff. Brad was not used to being looked down on by a boy his own age. He did not find it pleasant.

He was grateful to the Indians. They doubtless had saved his life. Yet he did not like the contempt he saw in Sabattis' eyes. *"He* might not find it easy to get along by himself in Boston," Brad thought.

Sabattis skimmed fat from the stewing kettle and put it in the frying pan. Before frying the trout he rolled them in cornmeal. "Just the way Ma does," Brad thought, watching him. "Or did," he sadly corrected himself. The certainty that he would never see his family again was strong within him. His thoughts were dark and gloomy as he lay there, held to his bunk by his weak ankle and the weakness of near starvation.

Sabattis brought the cooked trout in the frying pan to the bunk.

"Good!" he said, patting his stomach. It was the one English word Sabattis had known before Brad had met him.

Brad picked up the smallest fish in his fingers. Sabattis had not removed the head and had fried it so hastily that the outside was burned while the inside was nearly raw. "I could have cooked it better," Brad thought. "There must be a number of things I can do better than this Indian boy can. I bet he doesn't know how to milk a cow or do hard examples in arithmetic. He's probably never even heard of Latin. Doubt if he even knows how to read." Still, Brad had to admit that the Indian boy's accomplishments were of more value than his own up here in the Maine wilderness.

"But I'll show him I can learn the things he knows," Brad vowed. "Pa would want me to prove that a white boy can learn how to get along in the woods as well as an Indian." Even though Brad had given up hope that his father was alive, it still seemed important to him to act in ways that would have pleased him.

"Poor Pa!" thought Brad, and closed his lips tight to keep them from quivering.

7

Their Daily Bread

Chief Kineowa had said that Sabattis and Brad were brothers. Brad was sure the chief had not said that he was the younger brother. Brad did not think that Sabattis was a bit older than he was, yet the Indian boy certainly acted as if he were sure he knew more. Like an older brother, he told Brad what to do and scolded him for his awkwardness. But, like a brother, he took care of Brad until he was able to hop about the cabin on one foot, then cut a stout cane for him to use. Yet Brad was sure that Sabattis looked after him because he had been told to, not because he really liked him.

Sabattis taught Brad that certain kinds of lily bulbs were good to eat when boiled; that the knoblike ends of brakes were good eaten raw. There had been food in the woods, Brad learned, if he had known how to find it.

One day Sabattis showed Brad how to make a noose out of spruce roots. Brad hobbled out of the cabin and Sabattis taught him how to set a snare for rabbits or squirrels by fastening the noose to a low bush. It seemed good to Brad to be outdoors again. He made and set another snare by himself.

The next morning Brad found he had caught a plump rabbit. He was proud of the first food he had contributed, though Sabattis seemed to take it for granted. He made Brad understand that as soon as he was able and had learned a little more he would be expected to do his share in providing their food.

Tough, fine spruce roots made a strong fishline. Brad sat one afternoon in the sun outside the cabin and knotted into a long fishline the roots Sabattis had brought him. Sabattis had seemed surprised that Brad knew how to tie firm knots. "I really know more than he gives me credit for knowing," Brad thought. He was looking forward to going fishing the next day. "I'll show that Indian boy I can fish — I hope," he thought.

The next day was warm and sultry, even early in the morning. "Be better fishing if the sun stays behind the clouds," Brad thought.

The boys did not stop to eat before starting out. Sabattis did not care when he ate, Brad had discovered. He ate when he was hungry or when there was plenty of food on hand. Some days the boys feasted, other days they ate sparingly. Yet, after several weeks of living with Sabattis, Brad had gotten back flesh on his bones. Except for his lame ankle, he felt as well as ever. Now, naked to the waist like Sabattis, Brad limped along behind him. Each boy had a fish pole over his shoulder and a rabbit-skin pouch filled with angleworms hitched to his belt.

They walked upstream, keeping close to the river. Not far beyond the clearing, Sabattis knelt and tasted the water in his cupped hands. "No good," he said in English and added several sentences in Indian language.

Brad made out that Sabattis had decided that there were no fish in the river at this particular spot. "But how can you tell by tasting the water?" Brad asked, using both words and gestures.

Sabattis either did not understand or pretended not to. Brad suspected that the Indian boy did not often try to understand English. Brad had learned at least two Indian words to Sabattis' one word of English. Brad was sure that Sabattis believed that the Indian language, like Indian ways, was best.

They walked on. Sabattis stopped to taste the water a second time and shook his head. They walked quite a distance, and Sabattis made several tastings before he found water good to fish in. He was not willing to share it with Brad. He motioned for Brad to go farther upstream.

Brad followed Sabattis' example and tasted the water before fishing in it. The river water did not taste as good as spring water, but whether it tasted of fish or not, Brad could not tell. He baited the hook Sabattis had found for him — part of a bird's breastbone — and tied a small stone to his line for a sinker. Then Brad swung his pole, letting his hook sink until he felt it touch bottom, then raised his line a few inches and waited for a bite.

Brad watched the dragonflies skimming on the smooth water. He saw the widening circle a fish made when it came to the surface to feed on bugs and flies. There were fish here. Brad longed to catch one — any kind of fish as long as it was a big one. He would enjoy showing Sabattis that he did not have to be taught to fish.

A slight quiver of his line told Brad that a fish was nibbling at his bait. He yanked his line in and found that the fish had taken the bait. He had been too eager. He realized that he must be sure he had the fish hooked before trying to land it. He looked downstream to see if Sabattis had caught any fish yet. Brad could see no fish on the grass beside Sabattis. The Indian boy was standing as straight and still as a tree trunk.

Brad remembered the first time he had gone fishing. He had not been much over six. He had fished off one of the Boston wharves, and his father's hand had been over his on the line. His father had taught him a lot about fishing. Now, feeling another nibble, it was almost as if he again had his father's hand to guide him. He gave a skillful jerk to set the hook, then a quick swing with his pole, and a large speckled trout was on the riverbank beside him. Brad had caught the first fish. Sabattis was still just fishing.

"How Pa would have enjoyed fishing this river!" Brad thought. One of his recurrent pangs of grief dulled his joy at catching his fish. Then he became pure fisherman, thinking only of the ways and appetites of fish. He caught a tiny frog in his hands and used it instead of a worm for bait. With the frog he pulled in a slim pickerel, a beauty of a fish if he ever saw one. One, two, three, four, five, six fish joined the first speckled trout on the bank. Then the sun came out bright and the fish sought deeper, cooler water. Brad realized that the best fishing of the day was over.

Brad liked the look in Sabattis' eyes when he saw how many fish Brad had caught. The Indian boy had caught only four. Brad even had the biggest fish. It was a great satisfaction to him to prove that there was one thing he could do as well as Sabattis.

87

Sabattis tasted the water where Brad had fished. "More good for fish here," he said.

"It is not. It's just that I'm a better fisherman," Brad felt like saying. But he held his tongue. There were still too many things about living in the woods that Sabattis knew and he did not.

On the way back to the cabin, the boys stopped to eat their fill of blueberries. A recent rain followed by a warm sunny day had plumped them until some of them were as big as marbles. "Ma would have made a blueberry pie," Brad thought. He felt he would never eat one of Ma's pies again. Thoughts of his family kept weaving back and forth across Brad's mind. If he only knew what had happened to them, his sorrow would be easier to bear, he often thought. This not knowing made it worse.

That night, by firelight, Sabattis showed Brad how to make a muskrat lure. He whittled until he had made two thin strips of wood about four inches long and two inches wide. He put a piece of birch bark between them and tied them together securely with spruce-root twine. Then he raised the lure to his mouth and made a low, buzzing sound.

"The muskrat, he think another muskrat and come," he said in Indian language. "I do like this." He made the motion of grasping something quickly. "Muskrats fear Sabattis. I can catch many. Maybe white boy catch one."

Brad got the meaning of all Sabattis said. Brad was getting to be good at understanding Indian. He set to work now, making his lure. He was pleased that Sabattis was thinking of taking him muskrat hunting. Perhaps his skill in fishing had made Sabattis think he was good for something besides squaw work. He hoped so.

The next morning, though still midsummer, was chilly. Brad felt goose pimples rise on his arms as he and Sabattis went to the river soon after sunrise. Brad still wore his homespun trousers, but he had long since given up wearing a shirt. He was sure Sabattis thought that only a weakling would wear a shirt in the summer.

Sabattis chose a spot where tall grass grew by the river. He crouched down and motioned for Brad to do the same. I'll show you how to do this, his manner said as he raised the lure to his mouth and made a sound like a muskrat.

No muskrat seemed to hear. The boys waited and waited. Brad had a cramp in his leg and moved to straighten it. Sabattis gave him a black look that ordered him to keep still. The Indian boy was motionless except for his lips against the lure. "He's playing it like a fife," Brad thought, though the sound was so thin he could hardly hear it.

It was a buzzing sound that finally carried to the ears that were meant to hear it. A small furry animal drew near. At the right instant Sabattis' hand darted out, quick as lightning. He had the muskrat by the throat and pressed out its small life.

"Now white boy try," Sabattis said.

Brad made hard work of making a buzzing noise through the lure. Once, instead, he made the shrill sound one makes with a blade of grass. He could not seem to get the noise just right. Sabattis soon grew impatient. "You no can do. Me catch another muskrat," he said.

"I bet he didn't catch one the first time he tried," Brad thought, feeling that Sabattis was unfair in being so impatient with him.

It did not take Sabattis long to catch another muskrat. "Only Indians can do," he told Brad. "I have enough for today."

"I'm going to try it awhile longer," said Brad, gesturing to Sabattis to go back to the cabin without him. "Sabattis thinks I'm no good at hunting muskrats," he told himself. "Maybe so, but I'm not going to give up yet."

All the rest of the morning Brad crouched in the tall grass. Every few minutes he blew into his muskrat lure. Once he enticed one of the little animals, but when he tried to grasp it he found himself holding only empty air. His hand had not been quick enough. He tried again and failed. Again he tried. Still he had not caught a muskrat.

It was now past noon. The reflection of the trees in the river was so plain that the river almost seemed an extension of the forest. Trees were everywhere, even in the river. There were fat lazy clouds in the blue sky. Bees hummed in the clover. A white butterfly lighted on a tall spear of grass close to Brad's hand. The sun was warm on his back. He put his ear to the earth and it seemed as if he could hear the grass grow. He felt a sudden kinship with his surroundings as if he, too, were as much a part of the forest as a tree or a stone. It was a warm sense of belonging.

Again he lifted the muskrat lure to his lips and breathed through it gently. A small muskrat nosed its way toward the sound. Brad willed to grasp it, and this time his hand obeyed his will. He caught his first muskrat. This time his quickness was enough.

Full of pride, Brad took his muskrat back to the cabin. "You see a white boy *can* lure a muskrat," he said.

Sabattis looked surprised but pleased. "White boy small part Indian," he said, as if that were the only way to account for Brad's success.

"I'm not part Indian," Brad said hotly. Then he knew it was no use to argue with Sabattis. The Indian boy would close his ears; would choose not to understand. Besides, Brad did not feel insulted to be called part Indian. He realized that Sabattis meant it as a compliment.

The boys skinned their muskrats and put the meat into the stewing kettle. At first it had bothered Brad that Sabattis saw no need for washing the kettle after each meal. By now, Brad seldom washed it himself. If any meat was left in the kettle from the day before, so much the better.

Brad was so hungry after his day in the open that he could hardly wait for the muskrat stew to be done. As soon as the kettle was off the fire, he dipped in and brought out a piece of meat so tender that he was sure it was *his* muskrat. The joy of achievement gave it a special flavor.

8

The Bough House

The next morning Brad woke up sweating. Although it was still early, he could feel that it was going to be a hot day.

Sabattis was sitting beside him yawning. He had waked up feeling cross. "Cabin no good for sleeping in summer," he said to Brad accusingly. "Air bad. No can sleep. No can breathe."

"Why, you always sleep well!" declared Brad. He looked at the window hole and at the light coming through the cracks between the logs where he had not been able to reach to chink them. "There's plenty of air here."

"White boy weak because all year he live in cabin," said Sabattis. "Indian strong because summer he sleep

94

in bough house. Today white boy help Indian build bough house for sleeping."

"Right now I may not be as strong as you are but I will be soon," Brad vowed to himself. "Just because I was half-starved and helpless when you found me doesn't mean I'm still that way." He did not say this aloud. He had already learned that it was no use to argue with Sabattis. But he could not help saying, "I'm not too weak to catch fish or muskrats."

"The Great Spirit is sometimes kind to the weak," said Sabattis.

Brad felt like punching him, but he reminded himself that he owed a great deal to the Indian boy. Without Sabattis' care he would not be alive at all.

Sabattis lost his ill-humor once he and Brad were out in the woods, cutting fir boughs. The forest was cool, the shade deep. Fat tears of balsam ran down the trunks of the firs. The balsam looked colorless on the tree but turned to black pitch on Brad's arms and hands.

The fir smell was strong and good. Sabattis' quick nose caught another smell and he brushed aside some dead branches to find checkerberries just beginning to turn red. He picked a handful of leaves, which he shared with Brad. The boys chewed the leaves, finding the taste pleasant. "Once Ma made checkerberry tea," Brad remembered.

"The berries are good but not so much taste as the leaves," said Sabattis.

Brad's thoughts came back to the present. He and Sabattis dragged fir boughs out to within fifty feet of the cabin. They dropped them close to where Brad had planted corn and potatoes between the stumps. The corn was well up and the potato plants had blossomed. "We'll have potatoes to dig in another month or so," Brad told Sabattis.

Sabattis grunted. He did not seem to care. His concern was always today's food, not tomorrow's. Now he was interested only in building the bough house.

Brad thought they would use only fir boughs, but he found they also needed four birch saplings. Sabattis cut these and set Brad to stripping the leaves from the slim branches.

"What'll we use these for?" he asked Sabattis.

"To bind the fir branches together," Sabattis told him.

Brad could see that the tough birch twigs would be nearly as strong and flexible as wire. "There's everything in the woods a person needs if he knows where to look for it," he mused. He carried his stripped branches to where the fir boughs were heaped.

Sabattis cut from his belt a length of twisted rawhide. With this he tied the four birch poles together at the top. Then Brad held them upright while Sabattis spread the ends as far apart as possible on the ground, wedging them firm with stones. That was the framework of the bough house. Next Sabattis showed Brad how to lay fir branches tips downward along the supporting poles, binding them at intervals with the birch withes.

The boys worked hard. Long before night, their evergreen tepee was done. The air would circulate between the fir needles. Brad could see that it was a perfect summer shelter.

"Now I can sleep well nights," said Sabattis with satisfaction.

"Guess I'll sleep better, too," said Brad, though he, like Sabattis, usually slept like a log. But sleeping in the bough tepee would be fun.

The boys were so eager to try out their green tent that they went to bed before dark. Brad remembered what his mother would have said: "before it was dark under the table." They had fir boughs below and above them. They were cradled and sheltered by fir boughs. The perfume of the forest was strong in their nostrils. It was all very peaceful. But not for long.

"Today I have seen a small larch tree. Tomorrow I cut it and make strong bow for you. Now that you are a hunter, you need a bow," said Sabattis.

Brad felt a rush of pleasure. Catching the muskrat, he thought, had been a little like passing an examination at

school. He had proved his skill to the Indian boy, shown himself ready to hunt bigger game than muskrat — maybe a deer. Brad remembered that his father had told him not to shoot a deer before the family came. But they had not come. And now that Sabattis was with him, there would be two of them to eat the venison. Brad was pretty sure his father would have approved his going hunting for deer now. "When do we hunt the deer?" he asked Sabattis.

"When summer has been slain by winter and her blood has stained the leaves of the oaks and maples, we will hunt the deer," said Sabattis. "First you must practice much. But with arrows of your own making. My father gave me beautiful steel-tipped arrows. I will not risk them in your careless hands."

"Say!" cried Brad. "I'm getting mighty tired of your making out that I can't do anything and don't know anything. I'll tell you something you don't know. One day while you were out fishing, I stayed at the cabin. I pinned a piece of birch bark to a tree for a target. And I shot at it from just outside the cabin door and didn't hurt your bow or lose one of your arrows."

Brad spoke partly in English and partly in Indian. Sabattis understood most of what he said; enough to know that Brad had borrowed his bow and arrows without his consent. The Indian boy's eyes flashed with anger. "No right!" he screamed. "Bad! Wicked to take something not yours."

"I only borrowed them. I didn't hurt them."

Sabattis gripped Brad's arm so hard it hurt. "Touch them again and I will make you much sorry, white boy."

"If I hadn't lost my father's rifle I'd show you I know how to shoot," muttered Brad.

"You would shoot me?" cried Sabattis in a shrill strange voice.

"Of course not. I'd just show you I'm a good shot," said Brad. He had not thought Sabattis would mind his borrowing the bow and arrows. Brad suddenly recalled how angry *he* had once been when his little sister, Prudy, had made a nick in his treasured jackknife by whittling wood with a nail in it. "But I didn't hurt his old arrows," Brad argued with himself. Still, he had to admit that he might have lost an arrow.

"I shouldn't have taken your arrows," he said gruffly. "Should have asked you first."

Sabattis did not show he had heard Brad's words of apology. He rose from his bough bed and left the tepee.

"Where're you going? Come back. I told you I was sorry," Brad cried after him.

No answer. The Indian boy was gone. Brad was once more alone. He felt panic rise in him. He tried to re-assure himself by remembering that he would be in no danger of starving now that he had learned how to get his food from the forest and river. He was strong enough to take the rough fifty-mile walk down river. But there would be nobody who would care much if he came back from the woods. He had two uncles living near Boston, but he did not know them well. He would not want to go live with them. They might not even want him. Sabattis seemed closer to him, more nearly related. They had been alone together day and night for over a month. He knew Sabattis better than he did anybody else in the world, Brad realized, as he lay alone in the bough house he and the Indian boy had so happily built together.

It was true that Sabattis was sometimes aggravating, but Brad had grown fond of him. His company and their life together in the woods had helped ease Brad's sorrow for his family. "It takes two to make a quarrel." How many times Brad remembered his father's saying that. And what if Sabattis was quick-tempered. Brad had learned that the Indian boy's rage would come on as quickly as a summer storm and be gone as soon. "I wish I had left his bow and arrows alone," Brad mourned.

The green tepee no longer seemed a pleasant place to sleep in. Brad did not want to stay there alone. The wind played a sad tune in the pines. "Sabattis has gone, and I'm all alone again," said Brad's thoughts. Suddenly he could not bear to stay in the tepee another minute.

A waning moon in a dull sky feebly lighted Brad's way to the cabin. "I'll not stay up here in the woods by myself," he thought. Yet he was not ready to face life with strangers. He had been living one day at a time in the summer woods with Sabattis. He had not planned ahead. "I don't know what to do," he said. "I just don't know what to do."

Brad opened the cabin door. It was dark in the cabin. He groped his way to the bunk. And there lay a dark shape — Sabattis, fast asleep. He had not gone far.

Careful not to wake him, Brad lay down beside Sabattis and went to sleep with a thankful heart.

When Brad woke the next morning, Sabattis was at the fireplace, building a fire. Hearing Brad move, he turned around. "Today we make strong bow for you," he said pleasantly, as if he had forgotten the quarrel.

"Sabattis," said Brad solemnly, "I promise I'll never touch your bow and arrows again."

"If you speak true, there is now a clear path between us," said Sabattis gravely.

That was the end to the quarrel.

The boys spent most of the morning making Brad's bow. They cut a slim larch and removed the bark. Then Sabattis soaked the wood in water and held it close to the fire, bending the wet wood while warm. He worked slowly and carefully. Brad watched the wood yield to his will. The Indian boy gave the rest of his thong belt to make the bowstring. He did all the work of making the bow while Brad made the arrows, whittling them from branches of rock maple. It was slow work, for the wood was hard. He made them sharp. They would not be strong enough to kill a deer, but Brad hoped they would be sharp enough to kill small game.

Although Sabattis seemed friendly all day, when night came, Brad was not sure that the Indian boy would want to sleep with him. "Are you going to sleep in the bough house tonight?" Brad asked.

"It was built for me to sleep in," said Sabattis.

"Shall I stay in the cabin or go out there with you?" asked Brad.

"Maybe make white boy stronger to sleep in bough house," said Sabattis, with a hint of fun in his black eyes. "Maybe strong enough to be good hunter."

The boys went out into the starlit night together.

"You helped build the bough house. It is also yours," said Sabattis, as he stooped to go in.

The fir boughs were fragrant and the night was pleasant. There was a new feeling of comradeship between the boys now that they had quarreled and made up.

"I always wished I had a brother near my own age," Brad thought drowsily. "Now it's almost as if Sabattis is my brother. He's all the family I have."

9

The Honey Tree

The summer days passed quickly. By mid-August there were cold nights that were a foretaste of autumn. Brad and Sabattis still slept in the bough house. They found it pleasant, however, to lie in front of an open fire in the fireplace before they went out in the cold. At these times, Sabattis proved himself to be no mean storyteller. Although he spoke in Indian language, if he spoke slowly, Brad could understand most of what he said. He told tales of the mighty deeds of heroes of his tribe. Brad was sure the Indian boy often stretched the truth to the breaking point, yet it was fun to listen to him.

One night Sabattis told the story of the creation of the first Indian.

"One dewy morning when the sun was young," said Sabattis, "the Great Spirit walked the earth he had made. He walked beside a rushing river, which he had also made. He saw the birds and beasts of the forest, all the living things he had shaped, and he took pleasure in the work of his hands. But the Great Spirit knew he could create something better than the birds and the beasts. He wished to make a being to enjoy the fruits of his creation. He decided to shape the master of the earth and all that was on it — the first Indian.

"So the Great Spirit took clay and fashioned it into the shape of man. It was soft, like all clay before it is baked, so the Great Spirit put the clay man to bake while he went hunting. But the fire was hot, and when the Great Spirit returned, he found the clay man burned black. So he took the clay man in his hand and threw him into Africa, where, from then on, men were born black.

"Then the Great Spirit fashioned another man from clay. This time, because the Great Spirit was so very careful that his clay man should not be burned, he took him from the fire too soon. This second clay man was white and underdone. So the Great Spirit took the underdone white man in his hand and threw him far. And the underdone white man landed in Europe, where, from that time on, men were born white.

105

"Then the Great Spirit fashioned a third man of clay. And he took this man from the fire at the exact instant of doneness. Not burned, not underdone, but perfect Indian color. The Great Spirit was pleased with the work of his hands. He picked up this clay man gently and set him down in the forest of America. The Great Spirit dressed him like a hunter, and put in his hands a bow and arrows. He gave the woods, the waters, and all the birds and the beasts of the forest to this man, the first Indian. And they all belonged to the Indians until the white man came and took away much of the land," said Sabattis bitterly.

"Let's not quarrel about that now. None of my family took any land away from the Indians. At least, not that I know of," said Brad.

"My father says it is now too late to drive the white men from our land," said Sabattis. He says we must learn to live in peace with the white man. But it was all ours — the forests, the rivers, all this side of the big water." The expression in Sabattis' black eyes was proud and sad.

Brad sighed. He thought Sabattis' version of the creation was hard on both the white man and the Negro. Sometime he would tell Sabattis the Bible story of the creation, but the Indian boy was in no mood to listen now. He seemed to be brooding on all the wrongs done his race. Brad sympathized with him. Lately he was com-

ing to understand the Indian's point of view. America
had been theirs.

Another night Brad talked about his family to Sabattis.
He felt a need to talk about them.

"The hair of my little sisters was the color of ripe
wheat," he told Sabattis in Indian language. "They had
pink cheeks and eyes as blue as the sunny sky."

Sabattis was silent. He had no sisters to describe.

"My mother was not tall. She was thin and quick as a
bird. Her hair was brown but her eyes were blue. So
were my father's," said Brad.

"My mother is plump, not thin," said Sabattis. "By
her looks she shows that she always has had enough to
eat."

"But so had my mother. Just because she was thin
doesn't mean she hadn't had enough to eat," argued
Brad.

Sabattis was unable to understand how a woman could
be thin if she had plenty to eat. Brad gave up trying to
convince him.

Nearly every morning Brad woke up shivering. As
soon as the sun was high it would still seem summer,
but the night winds certainly were practicing for winter.
One morning Brad found a purple aster in bloom near
the spring, and he noticed goldenrod in bloom. As Brad
dipped his kettle in the cold spring water, he saw that

the berries on a nearby elderberry bush were turning red. When the red ripened into purple, autumn would be here.

By the time Brad had brought the brimming kettle of water into the cabin, Sabattis had the fire going. The heat was welcome in the morning chill of the cabin.

"I woke this morning with my mouth yearning for sweetness," said Sabattis, wiping a sooty hand on his deerskin breechcloth. "Let us go into the woods today and search for a honey tree."

Brad's mouth watered when he thought of honey. He had not had a taste of anything sweet since over two months before, when the bear had come into the cabin and eaten all the molasses. "I'm ready to start right now," he said with enthusiasm.

"We will set out after we have eaten and have rubbed our bodies with raccoon fat so we may slip easily between the trees," said Sabattis.

As Brad rubbed the rancid grease on his legs — he had long since cut off his trousers above his knees — Sabattis looked at the rags that were all that was left of Brad's clothes.

"Soon I must kill a deer for a skin to cover your nakedness," he remarked.

"When can we hunt one?" asked Brad, wishing Sabattis would lend him one of his steel-tipped arrows. Brad knew he would do well to stun a deer, let alone kill it, with his wooden ones.

"We must wait until the first frost to hunt the deer," said Sabattis. "While it is summer in the forest, Indians let the deer families live without fear. But summer will soon be over. It will not be long before we can hunt the deer."

Soon the boys were ready to set out. Both carried their bows and arrows, in case they should meet a live dinner of partridge or rabbit on the way home. They walked through the clearing and entered the deep shade of the forest where morning seemed to come later than in the clearing.

Both boys wore their dark hair bound back from their foreheads with bands of snake skin. Brad, like Sabattis, wore a bright feather stuck in his headband. He was so deeply tanned that he was Indian color. Like an Indian, he had learned to step lightly, hardly disturbing a twig.

"Little wild brothers, do not run from us as we enter the forest," Brad told the rabbits and chipmunks as they scurried across his path. "It is only when we return that you need fear us." Brad suddenly realized that he was not speaking in English but in the Indian language. It was even becoming natural to him to think in Indian.

Under the pines, the bunchberries had tight clusters of bright red berries. They looked good to eat, but Brad

109

HIS INDIAN BROTHER

had tried them and found little more than skin and a
stonelike seed inside each berry. Wild cranberries were
faintly tinged with pink. All plants that had flowered in
the spring and early summer had come to fruit and
berry. Yet bees and butterflies kept busy in the later
blooms. As the sun rose higher, a golden light sifted between the trees. The crisp air smelled of ripeness.

As he walked along, Brad suddenly wished he could
show his mother the forest this beautiful morning. In
his mind's eye he saw her in her Sunday black silk dress,
the cameo pin rimmed with pearls fastening the lace
fichu at her throat. Brad had lost track of time and had
no idea what day of the week this was, but as he thought
of his mother he was remembering a Boston Sabbath.
The twins looked like little rosy-cheeked ladies in their
crisp India muslin frocks. His father was wearing his
fine blue broadcloth coat. They were on their way to
church and the bells were ringing. "Come to worship.
Come to worship," they pealed. A glimpse of ocean showed
at the end of the street.

Brad stumbled over a root and his mind came back to
the forest again. He was used to recurring thoughts of his
family, though lately they had become less frequent.

Sabattis stalked ahead of Brad, humming a wordless
tune. Brad wondered how many generations of trees were
in the forest. Tiny seedlings grew beside dead logs. There

110

were trees of all sizes, and the tallest trees were older than
any living man. Brad was friends with the forest now. He
could slide through the branches almost as easily as
Sabattis. He no longer fought them. Nor did he feel lonely in the vastness of the woods now that Sabattis was with
him.

Sabbatis saw the honey tree first — a broken dead
trunk, kept from falling by the supporting branches of
neighboring trees. Bees buzzed around it.

"The honey's on the other side," Sabattis said in a low
voice, as if he were afraid of being overheard by the bees.

Dead branches lay thick around the tree. It was hard to
get over them. The boys scrambled around to the other
side. And there from the hollow heart of the tree came
the strong, sweet scent of honey. And the acrid, wild
smell of a bear and her cub, feasting on the stored sweetness.

Brad was thankful that Sabattis had brought along his
bow and steel-tipped arrows. He knew his feeble arrows
would not penetrate the hard hide of the bear. To his surprise, Sabattis did not raise his bow.

"Shoot it! You aren't going to let the bears have all
the honey, are you?" whispered Brad. "You can't miss.
It will be like aiming at a barn door." When Sabattis
still made no move to shoot the bear, Brad dared ask,
"Are you scared?"

Then two things happened at once. A bee stung the sensitive nose of the bear, and Sabattis sank one leg into an ant hill. He made a noise, and the bear turned around. Perhaps the bear blamed him for the fiery sting on her nose. Her eyes full of anger and hate, she lunged toward him. Sabattis was caught off balance. The angry she-bear would have been on him if Brad had not moved quickly. He picked up a dead branch and flung it in her face. Then, while the great beast vented its anger on the branch, growling and clawing it, the boys got away.

"We'll come back later," Sabattis said, when they were at a safe distance. "Though she is greedy, the she-bear will not take all the honey. When she has gone, we will get the rest."

"Why didn't you shoot the bear? She might have killed us both. You had plenty of chance to kill her," said Brad as they sat on a ledge to rest.

"We of the bear family never kill a she-bear," explained Sabattis. "It is the custom of my tribe. Many seasons ago when my forefathers were young, the small son of the chief was lost in the woods. A she-bear found him and took him to her cave. She kept him safe until his father found him. That is why my tribe became the bear family. That is why we do not kill the she-bear."

"Well, the she-bear didn't mind trying to kill *you*," said Brad.

Brad flung a branch in the mother bear's face

Sabattis unbound his quiver of arrows. He divided them, three for himself and three for Brad. "Half of my arrows are now yours," he said. "But you, too, since you are my brother, are therefore of the bear family and must not kill the she-bear."

A long look passed between the boys. Brad realized that Sabattis was thanking him for having saved him from the bear and for the first time was accepting him as an equal. It was a moment of deep meaning and satisfaction. Brad took his share of the arrows. There was no need for words.

Sometime later the boys went back to the honey tree. There were no bears in sight, and only half of the honey was gone. Plenty was left. Brad broke off a chunk of dripping honeycomb and sank his teeth in it. *"Umm!"* he grunted. "Never tasted anything half as good."

Most of the bees were away gathering honey. Brad was stung once on his forearm, but he hardly felt it, he was so busy eating honey. Sabattis, too, crammed his mouth with honey. The boys ate all they wanted and there was still some left. Sabattis made a crude basket of bark to carry the honey back to the cabin.

"There must be close to ten pounds," Brad gloated.

That night the boys feasted on fried mush and honey. They ate until they could not eat even one more waxy cell.

114

The moon was high as they went out to their bough house. It was so cloudless a night that all the stars were showing. Sabattis pointed out a number of bright stars. "There is the Great Bear," he told Brad. "It watches over the members of the bear family. It will protect you, my brother."

Brad gazed with awe at the faraway stars. He wondered what power the stars had on the earth. He knew that the moon influenced the tides. The stars might have a greater pull. Perhaps they kept the earth turning. Here was a mystery, something beyond knowledge. He looked in wonder into the immensity of the heavens.

As Brad went into the bough house, he gave a last look at the constellation of the Great Bear, the heavenly bear that watched over the bear family. It was his constellation now. He had the feeling of being guarded by the everlasting stars. Then he went into the evergreen tepee, lay down beside his brother Sabattis, and soon fell into peaceful sleep.

10

Escape

The golden days of late summer passed. The boys picked blackberries now instead of raspberries. Red stained the leaves of the vines along the riverbank. Frost flowers had the colors of spring but the ragged shapes of autumn. Sumac was dark red and velvety. The alders near the spring had bright red berries. Goldenrod was like gold lace trimming the dark woods.

One bright forenoon Sabattis shot a deer. The boys skinned it where it fell, cut up the carcass, and lugged meat and hide back to the cabin. For two days they feasted on boiled, fried, and roasted venison.

"We must smoke the rest of the meat before it spoils," said Sabattis at noon of the second day of their feasting.

Brad helped him cut the meat into strips. The boys built a fire outdoors on a low ledge near the river. The fire was close enough to the edge of the rock so they could hang the meat on slanting sticks driven into the earth beside the ledge. They were busy until dark tending the fire and turning the strips of meat. They kept the fire burning low, and often the veering wind blew smoke into their faces.

"It is good that the woods are not dry, though a fire on this ledge is safe if we watch it carefully," said Sabattis.

That night they went to bed smelling like smoked boys.

The deer hide meant new clothes for Brad. Sabattis showed him how to scrape the hide carefully with a sharp stone and stretch it between stout sticks to dry. To make the skin soft, Brad rubbed it twice a day for several days with raccoon fat.

One rainy afternoon the boys sat cross-legged on the cabin floor, making a breechcloth and moccasins for Brad. They sewed the hide with crude needles made from tiny bird bones with a hole at one end. The other end they had sharpened into a point. They used thin strips of rawhide for thread. For every stitch they took in the hide, a hole had to be punched with a sharp stick. Fortunately it took only a small number of stitches to make the clothing.

"This is squaw work," Sabattis complained. "I would

117

not have the patience to make hunting shirts and leggings for winter."

"Or the skill either," Brad felt like saying but refrained. Sabattis grew angry if criticized. The Indian boy never would acknowledge he could not do anything. It was always that he did not choose to do it.

Brad was glad to shed his rags and put on the breechcloth and moccasins.

"If one did not look too close he would think you were an Indian," Sabattis praised him.

Brad was pleased. He liked to be dressed like an Indian. Sometimes he thought he was beginning to feel Indian.

The rain stopped soon after Brad had put on his new clothes. Sabattis pinned a birch-bark target to a tree just outside the cabin, and the boys took turns shooting at it. Eight times out of ten Brad's arrow hit the target exactly in the center.

"How's that for shooting?" he cried.

"When I was ten years old I went into the forest alone with my bow and arrows and brought back a deer," said Sabattis.

"It must have been a pretty small deer. Anyway, I could have done the same if I had been brought up the way you were," said Brad. "I'm sure I could do it now."

"Then do so tomorrow, my brother," said Sabattis.

Brad shivered as he stepped out of the cabin early the

next morning, bow in hand, half of Sabattis' arrows at his waist. It was one of those crisp September days when the sun gave much light and little heat. The river was shrouded in morning mist. Before the sun was high the fishing would be good, but Brad turned his back on the river. Today he was hunting, not fishing.

He walked boldly into the forest. The crowding trees were no longer his enemies. They let him slip through their branches without bruising him. He stepped lightly, disturbing nothing, moving as one accustomed to the woods.

He was no longer afraid of getting lost. Sabattis had taught him how to tell direction by the thickness of bark on the trunks of trees, or by the veins of quartz, or the current of forest streams. If he failed to read all other signs, the setting sun or the stars would show him the way back to the clearing. Brad had learned his forest lore well. He could now walk in the forest without fear.

He heard beavers splashing about in a forest stream and caught a glimpse of their busy life. He heard the mournful *hoo, hoo* of a distant loon. Close to his head a slithering rasp was made by a milk snake shedding its skin against the thorns of a tall blackberry cane. He saw wild ducks winging their way south.

Brad found and followed a faint trail made by deer going to the river to drink. The path was so indistinct that

119

he kept losing and finding it. Soon he saw signs of deer — a nibbled sapling, hoofmarks on the soft forest floor. The trail wandered about among the trees. Brad followed it for a long time.

The sun was high when he broke out of the woods. There, not many feet away, was the river and a young buck drinking. Brad's breath quickened. Careful not to make a sound, he fitted an arrow to his bowstring. He aimed. The deer raised its head as the bowstring twanged. It leaped into the air and came down again. Brad saw its hind legs collapse slowly. It fell.

"The Great Spirit created deer for the Indians. They kill only as many deer as they need," Brad remembered Sabattis saying. That stilled his regret at having shot such a beautiful animal. Yet it was with mingled pride and sadness that he walked over to the dead deer and pulled out his arrow.

Brad hardly had the arrow in his hand when a shot rang from the woods. A bullet plowed into the buck's throat, only inches from Brad's hand. A large man in a red hunting shirt ran out of the woods. Behind him limped a dark-complexioned man with a face like a weasel.

"Got him with one shot," bawled the big man, advancing toward the fallen buck.

Brad stood his ground. "You shot at a dead deer," he

said. "You must have seen it was down before you shot. See? My arrow went in here."

The big man glowered at Brad. "It takes more than a pindling arrow to kill a buck. It's my deer and I shot it, and don't you try to tell me different. My bullet's in it, ain't it? Get back to your stinking tepee, you lying, thieving Injun."

"But I *did* kill it," Brad insisted, outraged at the big man's words. "You lie if you say you did."

The big man's bull-neck swelled. He put out a hand as large as a ham and gripped Brad by the shoulder. "I always did say that the only good Injun was a dead one. Wouldn't take much more for me to get really riled and take a shot at you, too, you dirty dog." He shook Brad until the boy's teeth rattled. Brad struggled and kicked but could not get loose. The big man's clutch was too strong.

The big man let go of Brad so suddenly that he nearly fell. Before he more than regained his balance, the weasel-faced man had hold of him and was staring at him as if he had been a captive wild animal. "Got gray eyes, this Injun has, Eph," he said to the big man. "Half-breed. Worse than skunks, they be. Hardly worth shooting."

"I'm no half-breed," cried Brad. "I'm as white as you are, but don't you say a word against the Indians. They're my friends."

121

"Is that so?" The weasel-faced man looked at Brad more closely. His strong skinny hand was around Brad's wrist like a vise. "How come you happen to be way off up here?"

Brad's only answer was a sullen look. He was not telling. For if rascals like these learned where the cabin was, they might claim it, as well as his deer. He knew he and Sabattis could not defend the cabin against men with rifles. These were two scoundrels, if he ever saw any.

"Maybe I took a walk up river and got lost," Brad told the men.

That remark brought him a painful box on the ear. "I don't like boys who act smarty — white or Injun," snarled the big man. "I'll give you a start while I count to ten and then singe your hair with a bullet. I won't cry if it hits closer."

"Not so fast, Eph," said the weasel-faced man in his whining voice. "Stands to reason if a boy's way up here, it's 'cause he's run away. I hear there're two or three bound boys missing from Bangor. Likely he's one of them. Remember, there be a reward for returning a bound boy to his master. I really think this boy be white. His cheekbones don't look Injun. Let's take him down river to Bangor."

"But what if he ain't one of the missing boys, Zeke?" asked the big man.

"I can get some work out of him on my farm," said Zeke, prodding Brad's arm with a bony forefinger. "He ain't got much meat on his bones but he looks wiry. A taste of the buggy whip and he'll be a good worker, or at least good enough to earn his keep. Boys and horses ain't a mite of good till they be whipped and let know who be their master."

Brad tried to pull away. The small man, Zeke, gave him a vicious slap on the side of the head. "We'd best tie him up, Eph," he said to the big man. "You've gone wild but I'll tame you," he threatened Brad. "You ought to be ashamed of yourself for living with Injuns 'stead of with decent white folks."

Many times in the lonely days before Sabattis and his father had come, Brad had longed to see a white man and dreaded to see an Indian. Now he thought how much more decent Sabattis and his father were than these brutish white men. It made Brad ashamed of his race.

Brad was helpless against the two men. They trussed him hand and foot and bound him to a tree. The big man tied the ropes cruelly tight but Brad set his teeth and endured the pain without a sound. These evil men, he knew, would be taking him to a miserable future. Somehow he must get away. When the men left him and walked to the dead deer, Brad strained at the ropes with all his might. He could not break or even stretch them.

Brad watched the men clumsily cut up the deer. They
made gashes in the hide as they skinned it. Their hands
were much less skillful with a knife than Sabattis' hands.
Brad himself could have done better. Soon they built
a fire to cook some of the venison. The smell of roasting
meat made Brad realize he was hungry, yet when the
men ate they did not even throw him a bone.

After their meal, the weasel-faced man drew a bottle

of rum from his pocket. The big man smacked his lips. "Just what I need. Give me my turn at the bottle, Zeke." The two men sat close to the deer carcass where the flies were gathering and passed the bottle back and forth, guzzling noisily as they drank.

When the bottle was half empty, they began to argue.

"If I was as big as you I could lick you with one hand tied behind my back," said Zeke.

"You could not. Stand up and I'll knock you down with my little finger," bellowed Eph.

"'Twouldn't be fair, for I ain't as big as you," argued Zeke. "And you can't say that ain't so."

"Guess you're right," Eph acknowledged, "but if I was as small as you, Heaven forbid, I still could beat the daylights out of you."

"You could not."

"I could so."

Brad hoped that a fight would develop, but the men did all their quarreling with their tongues. Their speech grew thick, their voices hoarse. It was Zeke who had the last drink from the bottle. His big companion had lain down and gone to sleep.

Zeke chuckled unpleasantly. "Proves I am stronger," he said thickly. He shied a rock at Brad before lying down beside Eph. Soon both men were snoring loudly.

Brad knew that his only chance of escape was while

they were in this drunken sleep. He had already found the ropes too strong to break. Somehow he must manage to untie the knots. Slowly and painfully he bent his head far enough down to reach with his teeth the knot that bound his hands. To untie the knot seemed impossible. His forehead grew wet with sweat as he worked at it. It took him a long time to loosen one strand ever so slightly.

"I'll bash your head in," shouted Eph. Brad froze. He did not move again until he heard the big man go on snoring and realized that Eph had spoken in his sleep.

At last Brad's hands were free. He had to rub the numbness out of them before he set to work to untie the other ropes. The men still slept. Wood ashes glowed where they had had their fire. Brad wished he dared stamp out the last spark before he left. It was carelessness of hunters like these that caused forest fires. Yet he could not risk waking the men from their drunken sleep. And Brad wanted with all his heart to escape from them and to return to Sabattis.

Stealthily Brad crept away. He drew a deep breath of relief when he had put a safe distance between him and the evil white men. Now he could go back to his Indian brother and live the clean, free life of the woods.

That night Brad told Sabattis what had happened, as they lay in front of a leaping fire in the fireplace. Brad talked in Indian language, which by now he spoke easily.

126

"They are bad men," he ended. "All white men are not bad, but these men are."

"You did well to escape from the white men," said Sabattis. "Much better you stay with me. I tell you something, Brad. I was not pleased when my father commanded me to stay here with you instead of going to the sea with him and other members of my tribe. Many members of my tribe live and fish by the sea in the summer. My father and I were on our way there when we stopped to cut birch bark for making a new canoe. Now I do not regret not having gone with my father. I do not mind staying here with you. At least not often," he added, not wanting to admit too much.

"I like staying with you, too," said Brad. "Besides," he went on, as shy as Sabattis about expressing affection, "your father expects to find me here when he comes back."

A companionable silence was between the boys. Brad went on thinking about his meeting with the white hunters. Now that he could think calmly, he realized that even if they had taken him to Bangor, Zeke could not have kept him slaving on his farm. Nor could anybody have proved he was a bound boy who had not finished his term of bondage. For there were people in Bangor who would remember him, Brad was sure. He and his father had stayed there overnight on their way

127

here from Boston. They had bought supplies at two Bangor stores. Somebody would remember them. He could prove his right to live as a free white man.

Here by the fire with Sabattis, Brad realized that one of the reasons he had wanted so desperately to escape from the white hunters was because he wanted to go on living with Sabattis. He did not want to go back to live with white men. Today he had made a choice. If the Indians wanted him, he would live with them.

The wood snapped in the fireplace. "I'm sorry I didn't bring back the deer I shot," Brad said to Sabattis.

"There'll be other days and other deer," said Sabattis kindly. "The autumn is still young. It is still many suns before my father returns. One day soon you and I will run with the moose. If you are strong enough, you may be adopted into my tribe as an Indian brave. If you are worthy, you may be my father's second son."

"Then I can go on living with you?" Brad's words were half a statement, half an anxious question.

"Where else would you expect to live if you were an Indian brave of my tribe?" said Sabattis. Yawning, he reached with a stout stick to separate the burning logs in the fireplace.

11

Fire!

Two days later Brad shot another deer. This time nobody disputed his claim to it. He was disappointed when he found the carcass too heavy to carry home on his shoulders. He had dreamed of bringing home a deer in this way, as Sabattis said he had done. Brad had to take it to the cabin a part at a time — first, hide and head, and then the cuts of venison. Sabattis was willing to help but Brad wanted to take care of his first deer entirely by himself. The Indian boy came along to watch and to give advice.

"Be careful. Don't cut a gash in the hide. Here is where you slice to get a good haunch of venison." Sabattis insisted on telling Brad exactly how to cut up the deer.

Sometimes Brad grew tired of being told how to do things.

Sabattis walked beside him as Brad struggled back to the cabin with a heavy load. Halfway, he put it down and rested for a minute.

"Did you really bring back a whole deer on your shoulders when you were only ten years old?" Brad asked.

"It was so many moons ago I may have forgotten," admitted Sabattis, "but my first deer had much wider antlers than yours."

"Maybe it's so many moons ago that you've forgotten how wide they were," remarked Brad, shouldering his load again.

"That could be so," agreed Sabattis with a good-natured grin. He enjoyed boasting but was seldom angry when Brad accused him of stretching the truth.

When the last load was at the cabin, Brad laid aside the meat they could use and cut the rest into strips for drying.

"Shall I help you smoke the meat?" asked Sabattis.

"No, I'll tend to it." Brad was still feeling the pride of ownership of his deer.

"Then I'll gather herbs and lily roots for the stewpot," said Sabattis. "And I know where blackberry bushes grow higher than my head. We've had so little rain lately that the berries won't be big but they'll be sweet. Today you provide the meat, and I'll go for small foods that please the tongue."

Sabattis stalked off into the woods. Brad had come to understand that there were times when the Indian boy wanted to stretch his legs and his spirit in the vastness of the forest. Brad had seen him look at the cabin walls as if they confined instead of sheltered him. He had stayed near the cabin several days now. Brad knew it would do him good to roam the woods alone. For Brad knew his Indian brother very well. They had grown so close that often one knew what the other was thinking without the need for words.

Brad built his fire close to the edge of the ledge not far from the cabin. He used birch logs because they burned slowly. Yet in order to keep the fire low but steady he had to do much shifting and poking of logs. When he was not tending the fire, he was busy putting strips of venison on the sticks that slanted over the glowing wood. The heat of the fire, added to the warmth of the day, made Brad sweat. The sun was as hot as if it had been July. This seemed like a misplaced summer day. Boston fishermen would have called it a weather breeder, Brad recalled. There had been mackerel sky at sunset the night before, but Brad could see no signs of rain now. It would be a good thing if it did rain, he thought, for the woods were dry and some fool hunters might accidentally set the forest on fire.

After two hours of tending his meat, Brad began to wish he had shot a smaller deer. He burned his fingers turning the meat, and a rising wind blew smoke in his face, making him cough. He felt as if he were being smoked and dried along with the meat.

When his wood was low, Brad went to the pile behind the cabin for more. He struggled back with four heavy birch logs, which he dropped quickly, glad to be rid of their weight. The fire had burned nearly to ash. Brad flung the biggest log on the glowing ashes.

He sat down on the ledge and fell to dreaming of the day Chief Kineowa would return and take him to live with the Indians. Brad imagined the ceremony of being adopted into the tribe. There would be a ring of Indians around a campfire. They would grunt their approval when Chief Kineowa told them that this white boy was worthy of being adopted into the bear tribe. Brad hoped that he, like Sabattis, would be made an Indian brave. For had not his shooting of two deer proved him to be a good hunter?

A tongue of flame rose from the embers and began to lick the log. There were protruding ends of cut branches on it. A few dead leaves clung to one of them. One leaf had an instant of beauty as it was lit by flame. The other leaves caught fire. A sudden gust of wind picked up a burning leaf and whirled it to a patch of grass. Brad saw little flames racing along the ground.

He ran and stamped out one spurt of flame, then another. There were always others. The grass fire grew as it rushed toward the woods. Brad ran to the cabin for water. He brought back a pailful, dashed it on the nearest blaze. He ran to the spring for more water.

Water sloshed against his legs as he raced back with the dripping pail. By then the fire had leaped into a bush of ground hemlock. There was a noise like the snapping of hundreds of firecrackers.

It took too long to bring water. Perhaps he could beat out the fire with a wet blanket. He rushed to get a blanket from the bunk and ran to dip it in the spring. Then he slapped at the burning ground hemlock. There was the smell of scorched wool as he beat at the flames. They were too strong for him.

He saw a fir tree close to the cabin light like a candle. Just then Sabattis came running from the woods.

"Get water," shouted Brad. "I'm going to take wet blankets to the roof of the cabin. I must save the cabin."

"Let the cabin burn," cried Sabattis angrily. He grasped Brad roughly by the arm. "You have loosed the fire which will destroy the forest," he screamed in a voice shrill with rage. "My people will freeze this winter with no

133

wood for their campfires. They will starve because all the animals in the forest will be destroyed. The Indians befriended you and you bring them sorrow. They will call you 'He-who-set-the-woods-on-fire.' "

Brad pulled himself away. "I must save the cabin," he repeated.

"The fire is a giant. It walks with great steps you cannot stop," said Sabattis.

Brad paid no attention. He hurried to the spring to wet his blanket again and climbed to the cabin roof. A few glowing sparks were already landing on it. He beat them out. He heard the fire around the cabin roar like an angry sea. He saw it leap from tree to tree.

He needed to wet his blanket again. He climbed down to go to the spring. Then he saw that he could no longer reach the spring. Along the narrow path the trees were all in flames. The air was hot with the breath of fire. Sabattis had been right, Brad realized. The fire was too big for him to stop.

Sabattis ran out of the cabin, carrying their bows and arrows. "We must get to the river," he said in his usual voice. "It is our only chance."

The boys had to pass through a short but dreadful aisle of burning trees. The fire had spread beyond the grass near the river, but the ground there was still hot. It blistered the boys' bare feet. They reached the river and waded out until the water was up to their shoulders. The fire could not reach them now, though the wind blew blazing twigs into the water near the shore.

"The animals, too, are coming to the river," said Sabattis, pointing.

Brad saw many small animals run from the burning woods — rabbits, porcupines, skunks, chipmunks, squirrels. And the larger forest animals — deer, moose, bears, wildcats. They all sought the safety of the river. Soon they were splashing in the shallows near the boys. Natural enemies stood peacefully side by side. They trembled with fear, but not of one another. The fear in their eyes was of the fire.

"Their homes are being destroyed," Brad thought sadly. And because of the fire, he, too, would be homeless. For the cabin would be burned, and if the Indians blamed him for the fire, they would not let him live with them. His family were dead, and Sabattis hated him. Nobody in the world would care if he lived or died.

"If you hate me so much why didn't you run to the river without me? You waited for me, didn't you?" Brad asked Sabattis.

"I promised my father to look after you. I keep my promises," said Sabattis stiffly.

"Perhaps the fire was a little my fault, but it's not fair to blame it all on me," said Brad. And he told Sabattis

135

how the fire had started — the wind, the flaming leaf, the dry grass.

Sabattis did not speak until Brad had finished. Then he said, "In anger I spoke harsh words to my brother. Now I see that the fire was not his fault. For some reason the Great Spirit is angry and sent the wind to blow the burning leaf."

The wind fanned heat from the fire against Brad's face. At the same time he was chilled by the cold river water. He had never been much more miserable in body, yet his mind was greatly relieved now that Sabattis was no longer angry with him. The wind strengthened. If it kept on blowing, miles of forest would be doomed. Brad mourned for the trees that were being consumed by fire.

Beside Brad, Sabattis was murmuring a prayer to the Great Spirit. Watching the fire attack the helpless trees, Brad felt the need to pray, too.

"Dear God," he prayed, "save the forest. The deer and the moose and the Indians will be homeless without it. And if it be thy will, save my father's cabin. And Sabattis and me. Amen."

For over two hours Brad and Sabattis stood in the river. The sun had gone in or was shrouded in smoke. All the glare and bright light were from the fire. Brad wished that a miracle would make the river change its course and rush into the woods and put out the fire. But

The animals ran from the burning woods, seeking safety

he knew a river went its own way. Each thing in nature was indifferent to every other.

"How I wish I had ripped off those leaves before I put that stick of wood on the fire!" Brad thought. Sabattis no longer blamed him, but he still blamed himself, though he knew it was an accident that had caused the fire.

"Both of us should have known that the woods were too dry to build a fire outdoors," said Sabattis.

It was as if Sabattis had read his mind and was taking part of the blame, Brad thought gratefully. He had never been fonder of his Indian brother than he was at this minute.

A burned tree fell. Crows cawed, scolding the fire. Suddenly Brad felt a wetness on his cheek that was neither river water nor tears. It had begun to rain.

"The Great Spirit heard my prayer," cried Sabattis joyfully.

"I prayed, too," said Brad. "Oh, let it rain, let it pour! I don't care if I half drown if only it rains hard enough to put out the fire."

There was a cold bite to the wind now. The rain pelted down fast and hard. The boys raised their drenched faces and watched it pour onto the burning forest. Soon they saw the fury of the fire begin to subside. Then, so numb with cold they could hardly walk, they waded back to shore.

"If only it will keep on raining!" Brad cried, his wish a sort of prayer.

The cabin had not burned, though the trunks of the trees close to it were blackened. Brad thought that he had saved it, for he had put out flying sparks on the roof. Where the bough house had been, there were only ashes.

"It was getting to be too cold to sleep in the bough house," said Sabattis. "This is the storm that marks the end of summer. It came in time to save the forest. The rain is good."

This must be the line storm, Brad thought. He had lost track of time. It must be somewhere near the third week in September. There was always a big rain then. Thank God this one had come when it did!

Clouds of steam rose from the forest. The fire was dying out fast. The boys were so thankful for the rain that they stayed out in it until dark. Then they went inside the cabin and ate their supper cold. Even though they were still chilly, they could not bear just yet to build a fire. Fire could be a friend, but it too recently had been a deadly enemy.

With great satisfaction, the boys heard rain beating on the roof. They squatted before the cold hearth and did not mind when water came down the chimney hole and fell in the ashes.

"Rain is good," Sabattis said again.

"I hope the fire wasn't really my fault." Brad was still uneasy in mind.

"The fire is out, so nobody is to blame for it," said Sabattis.

And although the Indian boy's remark did not make much sense, Brad found it oddly comforting.

12

To Run with the Moose

There were golden Indian summer days in October; bright mornings when the river shimmered with light. There were cold, gray days, with the river slate-colored. Sharp winds tore the last autumn leaves from the oaks and the birches. Mornings were always cold. Before a brisk fire warmed the cabin, the boys could see the smoke of their breath. Often the grass outside was stiff with frost.

On the coldest days the boys wore deerskin hides tied across their backs. They needed hunting shirts and leggings, but their skill at sewing was not equal to making them. Most of the time their young blood and their coat of tan kept them warm. And they were constantly on the move when out of the sun or away from the fire.

One bright, frosty morning Sabattis looked at the sky to read the weather. "The day will be fair and the hunters' moon bright in the evening," he remarked. "Today let us run down a moose. Did you know, my brother, that a man cannot become a chief of my tribe unless he has run down a moose?"

"Isn't a moose hard to chase?"

"Naturally. But to run down a moose is the test of a great hunter. We must follow the moose wherever he leads. Even if we run after him all day we must keep on until he tires. For we must show the moose that we are stronger than he is. He must know this before we send our swift arrows to kill him."

"Will we both shoot at the same moose?" asked Brad.

"Unless you prefer to chase a moose by yourself," said Sabattis. "I had thought we would hunt together."

"I'd rather hunt together," said Brad quickly. "I got chased by a moose once, so now it's my turn to do the chasing."

Brad had told Sabattis about his experience with the cow moose and had been relieved that Sabattis had thought none the less of him for climbing a tree to get away from the angry animal. Sabattis had said that any Indian would have done the same if threatened by a moose protecting her young.

"We hunt a bull moose, not a cow moose, today,"

142

Sabattis remarked. "This is the time of year for hunting moose. But before we start we must make moose-calls out of birch bark."

The boys ripped off thick sheets of birch bark and cut two squares about a foot long and wide. Sabattis showed Brad how to roll his square of birch bark into a cornucopia and hold it in place with a thong of rawhide. Then, after Sabattis had made his moose-call, he taught Brad how to make the right noises to entice a moose.

"If you hear the moose near you, you grunt like this." Sabattis made a low, grunting noise, with his moose-call level with his lips. "But if the moose is far away, he can hear this better." And Sabattis pointed his moose-call downward and made an ear-splitting squeal.

"The moose thinks it's another moose," he said. "It also helps if you can feel a little like a moose."

Chilly though the morning was, the boys went into the forest clothed only in their deerskin breeches. They had smeared their bodies with muskrat grease, but that did not keep out the cold. Goose pimples rose on Brad's arms. After he had jogged along awhile, he felt warmer.

The boys slipped through the underbrush, hardly snapping a twig. They were deep in the woods before Sabattis squealed through his moose-call. They waited, but there was neither sight nor sound of a moose. Then Brad tried his moose-call, and then both boys made their moose-calls squeal together. Still no moose.

"The moose stays very deep in the woods," said Sabattis. "We must go farther."

When the sun was overhead, the boys stopped to eat some dried venison and to drink from a brook.

"Drink only a little," Sabattis advised Brad. "For when we find a moose we will have to run far and fast. Drinking much water is not good for a person's wind."

They paused only a few minutes. Soon they were walking again — listening, calling, listening. Now and then they talked.

"I guess a bull moose is bigger than that cow moose I saw," said Brad. "And she looked 'most as big as a house."

"A moose is the largest animal in the forest," said Sabattis. "Moose used to be whales, you know."

"You're just making that up," said Brad.

"I speak only what I have been told is true," said Sabattis. "They *were* whales long ago. But a certain family of whales got tired of living in the ocean and came to live on land. On land, it is more convenient to have legs, so they grew legs. Soon after that they became moose instead of whales. The biggest whale turned into the king of the moose. He is said to live in the woods even now. My uncle had a glimpse of him once. He is as tall as a small mountain and his antlers are as wide as the branches of a giant pine."

"A moose couldn't be that big," protested Brad.

"How do you know? It was my uncle who saw him, not you," said Sabattis.

The boys stopped talking and sounded their moose-calls again. And not even an echo answered.

"You don't make the right noise," Sabattis complained. "Try to sound more like a moose or like his cousin."

"Who's the moose's cousin?" asked Brad.

"Another moose, of course," said Sabattis with a hint of a chuckle.

A startled deer ran from them. They found many signs of deer. Then Sabattis saw tracks he thought had been left by a moose. "Walk softly," he whispered to Brad. And the Indian boy raised his moose-call and grunted through it.

There was an answering sound.

The boys quivered with excitement. They managed to stand motionless, however, as the moose approached them. First they caught a glimpse of dark brown hide. Then the moose was near enough for them to see his broad chest and powerful body. The spread of his antlers was nearly as wide as the boys were tall.

The moose caught sight of them and snorted. Brad saw his startled eyes before he leaped and ran. The boys ran after him.

It was the beginning of a long race through the forest.

145

When the moose swerved to the right, so did the boys. When he backtracked, so did they. Wherever he turned and twisted between the trees, they followed. Once the big animal turned his thick neck to look back at his pursuers. Then he made such a spurt of speed that they nearly lost him.

Brad was a good runner, and his life in the woods the past few months had hardened him. Yet there came a time when running after the moose stopped being fun and became a matter of painful endurance. His heart pounded, his legs ached, he had a sharp pain in his side, and every breath he drew hurt his chest. But until Sabattis gave up the chase, neither would he. Brad ran on and on until his body begged him to stop and only his will kept him running.

Farther and farther the moose led the boys into the woods. Here the forest was so dense that neither they nor the moose could go fast. And Brad had a chance to recover his breath before the moose gave a new spurt of speed.

Through the long afternoon the boys ran with the moose. Sometimes he was almost hidden by underbrush. Once, when Brad glimpsed him beyond a fallen tree, the moose looked so huge that for an instant Brad had the illusion that this must be the very moose Sabattis' uncle had seen, the king of the moose himself. If it were a moose

The moose ran farther and farther into the woods

spirit they were chasing, he might run them to death. Then Brad shook off his superstitious fear. This was a real animal, an actual moose. And, like humans, he could tire.

"But the moose has four legs and Sabattis and I only two, so we get tired in half the time," Brad thought wearily. He saw that Sabattis was still running easily. "I'll keep on as long as he does," Brad vowed. "I'll run until I drop."

It was close to twilight when the moose stopped running and stood still. He lifted his head.

"He sees us," whispered Sabattis, and fitted an arrow to his bow.

Brad's fingers were shaking as he raised his bow. Then tiredness suddenly left him. His hand was steady and his aim was true. His arrow sped through the air at almost the same second as Sabattis'. The two arrows struck the wide chest not six inches apart. The big animal gave a leap, then fell heavily.

"The foolish animal could have outrun us if he had not become afraid," said Sabattis. "When we would not be left behind, he grew frightened. It was his fear that made him lose the race. He knew before he died that man is master of all the animals of the forest. Moose know that but they forget. It is well to remind them."

The boys gazed with pride at the dead moose. They

had had a contest with a creature several times their size and had won.

"Only great hunters ever run down a moose," said Sabattis. "My father will be pleased with me. And with you, too," he added generously. "If you had been a full-blooded Indian you could not have run better or shot more truly."

Brad flushed with pleasure. He was glad he had kept his legs going. "Guess I could outrun a moose most any time but I wouldn't want to do it too often," he said.

The sun was low. It was already dusk in the woods. The boys were a long way from the cabin. "It's too late to go back to the clearing. We will sleep in the woods tonight," said Sabattis. "Help me skin the moose, my brother. The skin and antlers we must save to prove to my father the great size of this moose we ran down and killed."

The woods were dappled with moonlight before the boys finished skinning the moose. The night air had frost in it. The boys pushed back the cold a few feet by building a fire. They stood close to it and cooked tender pieces of moose meat hung from the ends of sticks. The meat was a little tougher than venison but tasted good.

The woods were so damp that it was safe to keep a fire burning all night. The boys piled fir boughs for their bed as close as they dared to the fire. Then they crawled in among the balsam needles, which were both mattress and blanket. They lay close to each other for warmth, but Brad was still too cold to sleep. At last, shivering and aching with cold, he got up and put another log on the fire. Then he jumped up and down to warm his blood.

The moonlight was very bright. "October moons always seem the largest of all the year," Brad thought, looking up at the silvery disk high in the sky. The moon shone on a nearby ledge and made the mica in the rock sparkle like diamonds. The cold, clear light touched the forest with mystery. An owl hooted. There were rustlings in the woods, the sound of snapped twigs. The antlers of the dead moose looked like a leafless branch. What if other moose came to avenge their dead king, Brad mused. He put more wood on the fire. He could get only one part of him warm at a time.

"Why are you not sleeping?" Sabattis stood near him, his voice drowsy.

"I was too cold to sleep."

"I, too, am cold," said Sabattis. "Go back and lie down. I will bring a blanket to keep us warm."

Wondering what Sabattis meant, Brad went back to his bough bed. He saw the Indian boy dragging something toward him. It was the moose hide. Hairside down, it was a warm covering.

Brad soon fell asleep. He dreamed of a giant moose

as tall as a mountain and with antlers that reached the sky.

"It is my turn now to chase you," the moose said, and Brad saw he had a crown on his head. "You must run fast or I shall overtake you."

"Stop kicking me," Sabattis complained.

"I had a queer dream," said Brad, waking up.

"This is no time for telling dreams," grumbled Sabattis and was immediately asleep again.

Brad saw that the moon had set. The stars now shone more brightly. They were farther away but seemed friendlier than the moon. Brad found it pleasant to look up at them and think how he had passed the test of a great hunter. Sabattis had said that no man could be an Indian chief until he had run down a moose. Brad hoped the time would come when he would be a chief. He hoped he would be brave, and strong, and wise. Like his own father and like Chief Kineowa, who might adopt him as his second son. Then he and his Indian brother, Sabattis, would hunt and fish together for many, many moons. And always the constellation of the Great Bear would be their guiding stars.

13

Chief Kineowa Returns

One morning Brad's fingers were so numb with cold that he could hardly break kindling to coax the embers in the fireplace into flames. Sabattis came and squatted down and blew on the glowing ashes while Brad pushed in his light sticks and pieces of bark. The fire soon leaped and crackled. It was a welcome spot of light and warmth on a dreary November morning.

"My father will return soon," said Sabattis.

Brad had to break ice in the pail before he could pour water into the kettle to make their cornmeal porridge.

"The cornmeal is nearly gone," he said. "I ground all but the last two ears of corn yesterday. And we're down to the last four potatoes from the garden."

152

"No matter. More than four moons have passed. Before the river freezes, my father will come for us. After the river freezes, the canoe must be put to rest until spring. My father will come for us in his birch-bark canoe. He will take us up river where my tribe have their winter village. In the log houses of my people we will pass the winter. In the evening around the fire we will listen to the tales of old warriors and skillful hunters. My father will ask me, too, to speak. I will tell them how we have kept to the old ways but have fared well these months alone in the forest."

"What do you mean by old ways?" asked Brad. He stirred the coarsely ground cornmeal into the boiling water.

"Most Indians hunt with a rifle now instead of with bow and arrow," said Sabattis. He rose to his feet and stretched and yawned. "My father wished me to prove that men can live by the old ways," he said. "I have passed the test. So have you, though I had to teach you. We have eaten well from what we have obtained from the forest. And we have meat and hides to take up river to the Indian village as our share of food for the winter." Sabattis gazed with pride at the pile of deer hides in one corner of the cabin and the strips of dried venison hanging beside the door.

"We've been as busy as squirrels gathering nuts," said.

Brad. He wished the porridge were done. The cold air made him hungry.

"Men must do their hunting before the deep snows of winter," said Sabattis. "A time soon comes when only the icy winds can walk the forest paths. Hear the wind howl! Soon the vast whiteness of the snow will come."

Sometimes what Sabattis said sounded almost like poetry, Brad thought. He marveled that the Indian boy could talk like this, especially before breakfast. "I certainly hope your father will get here before the first hard snowstorm," he said.

The porridge was done. Brad took the kettle from its hook and put it on the hearth. The boys dipped in their wooden spoons and blew on the porridge to cool it. Brad did not mind if it burned his tongue a little. Sabattis seemed to be able to eat almost anything nearly red-hot, so he could eat his porridge faster than Brad. He talked to Brad while he finished eating.

"In the full of the moon the wind will be stilled and the river will freeze deep," said Sabattis. "Then the wind will rise and the snow will fall, and in all the woods there will be a great silence."

"How do you know? How can you tell what the weather will be?" asked Brad.

"How do the squirrel and the muskrat know when they must grow heavy fur before a cold winter? How did the birds know when to fly south? Like them, my feeling tells me. But my father will come for us before the river freezes and the deep snow comes. He will return today or tomorrow." Sabattis spoke with as much assurance as if he had just received a message from his father.

Brad found himself remembering the lonely days of longing for *his* father to come. He hoped nothing would happen to prevent Sabattis' father from coming. Yet he knew that even if he and Sabattis had to stay here alone all winter they would get along all right. Brad believed that together they could get along anywhere.

Chief Kineowa did not come that day. There were a few snow flurries in the morning of the next day. It stopped snowing before the snow was as deep as frosting on a cake. The sky remained gray, the air cold and damp.

At noon the boys sat before a roaring fire, the stewpot between them. Brad had just reached in for a choice piece of boiled venison when the cabin door opened. A blast of cold air rushed in as the deerskin that hung over the doorway was pushed aside.

"I greet you, my children," said Chief Kineowa, coming toward the fire. "Let me share the meat in your kettle, for I have been paddling since before dawn and have not stopped for food."

Joyfully, the boys made room for him.

The tall Indian looked every inch a chief, Brad thought,

admiring his strong features and dignified bearing. And today he was dressed like a chief. He wore a hunting shirt and leggings of soft doeskin. The shirt was richly embroidered with purple and white shells. His belt was of purple wampum, and around his neck was the necklace with dangling bear claws which Brad remembered.

Chief Kineowa put his lean, strong hand into the kettle and drew out a dripping piece of meat. He ripped into it with his teeth, not speaking until he had stripped it to the bone.

"The meat in your stewpot is tender. Deer, no doubt," he said politely.

"It is deer and squirrel and raccoon and muskrat and rabbit," said Sabattis proudly. "All of these within six suns have gone into the stewpot."

Chief Kineowa licked his long fingers. Even this he did with dignity. "A rich mixture makes the best stew," he said approvingly.

Chief Kineowa had brought a rolled bundle into the cabin. Now he opened it. He had presents for the boys — hunting shirts and leggings of deerskin. "Your mother sewed them," he told Sabattis.

The boys put on their new clothes at once. The soft leather felt good against Brad's skin.

"These clothes will keep in the warmth and keep out the cold," said Sabattis. "I will have my mother embroider

the emblem of our tribe at the neck of our shirts."

Chief Kineowa looked at the boys searchingly. "When two live together with no other person near, these two become either enemies or brothers," he said. "Your faces tell me that there is a clear path of friendship between you."

"We are as brothers," said Sabattis gravely. And Brad's heart warmed at the words.

Chief Kineowa looked about the cabin. He saw the pile of hides in the corner, the dangling strips of dried meat. "I saw several quarters of venison hanging outside where it is cold enough to keep the meat from spoiling," he said. "I see you have provided food for yourselves and to spare; food for the present and for the future. As in the days of our fathers, you have hunted quietly with bow and arrow and have not startled the forest with loud shooting. You have done well, my son."

Sabattis did not smile, yet he showed he was pleased.

"I can see that your white brother has entirely recovered from his hurt ankle," said Chief Kineowa.

Brad's ankle had been well for so long that he had all but forgotten it had been hurt. He wriggled it as he saw the chief glance at it.

"When I saw your white brother four moons ago he was as lean as a she-bear in the spring after a winter's fast," said the chief to Sabattis. "His spirit burned low as a dying fire, and he looked soon to become a lost, unhappy ghost. Now I see he has the flush of health on his cheeks. He has grown broader and taller. The forest has been good medicine for your white brother."

Brad began to wish that Chief Kineowa would stop

talking about him as if he were not there.

"My white brother is now like an Indian," Sabattis told his father. "In the beginning of my stay with him he was almost as a papoose. He knew not how to fish or hunt. He was a stranger to the woods. Like the new-born of some animals, his eyes seemed not open to what was there for him to see."

"I couldn't have been quite as bad as that," Brad protested.

Sabattis paid no attention. "I taught him many things," he said. "He was not slow to learn. That I will say of him. And now," Sabattis went on, his voice rising with enthusiasm, "my white brother has become my equal in the hunt. He is at home in the forest. He is as one of us."

"I rejoice that, like a young tree with its foot in fertile soil and its head in the sun, your white brother has flourished," said Chief Kineowa. He turned to Brad. "Now what do you wish, younger brother?" he asked. "If you so wish it, Sabattis and I will take you down stream to your white brothers. We will do this even though it will mean that he and I will have to pass the months of the long cold in Old Town instead of on the Indian island upstream which is our winter home. For the river will soon be locked in ice and will not be released until spring. There are some of the bear tribe in Old Town, so we will not be among strangers. And you

159

will be in the nearby town of Bangor among those of your own race."

Brad was touched that Chief Kineowa was willing to go to so much trouble for him. But he had no desire to be taken to Bangor. He would much prefer to live with the Indians. Yet he was too proud and shy to ask Chief Kineowa to take him to live with the bear tribe.

Sabattis spoke for Brad. He told his father that he had promised his white brother he would be adopted into the bear tribe. "He will be a good Indian," Sabattis said. "And he has passed the test of a great hunter." Sabattis then showed his father the moose's antlers.

"My white brother and I ran with the moose," he said. "Many hours and many miles we ran, and my white brother did not weaken. We ran the moose down. Then both our arrows flew at the same instant, and we killed him. My white brother and I killed the largest moose in the forest. Before he died, the giant moose knew that we were stronger than he and that he could not escape from us."

Chief Kineowa gave Brad a long look. Then he gave a grunt that signified that he approved of him. It was as if he had measured the white boy with his eyes and found him large enough in body and in spirit. "I take you by the hand in friendship," the chief said, grasping Brad's hand firmly. "The tongue of Sabattis can be believed.

In ceremonies around the campfire you shall be adopted into the bear tribe. You are my son's brother and will be to me a second son."

"That is what I want to be," said Brad, deeply moved. "I hope you'll never be sorry you've adopted me." Brad felt that he would learn to love and respect this tall Indian chief almost as much as he had his own father. Though they did not look alike, there was something about the two men that was the same — a strength, a quiet dignity. "I must never be cowardly or mean," Brad thought. "I must try to be worthy of being Chief Kineowa's second son."

Now that Brad's future was settled, they all relaxed. Sabattis boasted of his hunting, told how he and Brad had speared salmon in the river, spoke of the honey tree, and of how Brad had saved him from the she-bear's fury. He told his stories well, and his father listened and watched the fire.

When Sabattis had finished, Chief Kineowa asked, "What shall we call your white brother? What Indian name shall we give him?"

A look of sly fun came over Sabattis' face. "For many suns my white brother was lame. Why not call him Lame-foot?"

Brad was indignant. What a poor sort of name that would be for the second son of an Indian chief! "My real name is Bradford Cunningham Porter," he said loudly. And that really would always be his name, he thought, no matter what other name he went by. For a name given you at birth is yours to keep. Yet he wanted an Indian name. But one to be proud of, not a mean name like Lamefoot.

"Any boy who can run down a moose is fleet of foot," said Chief Kineowa. "Let us call him He-who-runs-like-the-wind."

"It is a true name for him," agreed Sabattis. "Lamefoot is what his old self might be called, but now he can run as fast as the wind."

Brad was content with his new name. He liked the sound of it in Indian language. And he liked what it meant and the picture of himself it suggested, a boy who moved quickly in the direction he chose to go.

"Tonight we stay here," said Chief Kineowa. "Tomorrow my swift canoe will part the gathering ice in the river. By nightfall we will reach the island where the campfires of our tribe burn bright. Then, like our brothers the bears, we shall not walk the forest trails again until spring."

While the chief rested from his journey, Brad and Sabattis began to get ready for their trip up river. They made a pile of dried meat and fish on the cabin floor, ready to be taken out to the canoe in the morning. The deer hides they took outdoors and stacked beside the canoe on the riverbank.

It was still afternoon, yet the early dusk was gathering. Brad looked back at the cabin and saw the plume of smoke rise from the chimney hole. He thought of the many heavy stones he had lugged for the chimney. It would never be built now. Brad suddenly wondered what would become of the cabin after he went to live with the Indians. He did not like the idea of leaving it for good.

"Can't you and I come back here and stay awhile next summer?" he asked Sabattis.

"I think not," said Sabattis indifferently. "We of the bear tribe often go to the sea while the space is long between the rising and setting sun. We do not return to the forest until after the days and the nights are equal, except to hunt."

The cabin meant nothing to Sabattis, Brad realized. He had not helped build it, or spent hours chinking the logs with clay. It was not Sabattis' father who had hacked the clearing from the wilderness. Brad sensed that this place held a meaning for him that the Indian boy would not understand. For even though Brad had finally accepted the belief of his father's death, there was much here which reminded him of his father. So often Brad had found himself thinking, "This, Pa and I did together. . . . Pa showed me how to do that." Brad had a feeling that memories

163

of his father would grow fainter once he left the cabin. He wanted to go, yet he felt a pang of regret.

"When my father is rested from his journey, he will be hungry again," said Sabattis. "I'll return to the cabin and set the kettle to boil. It was you who set the snares yesterday. If you have caught a plump rabbit in one of them, it will improve our stew."

Sabattis went back to the cabin while Brad went to inspect his snares. The first snare he looked at was empty. In the second, the thong slip noose tied to a low branch had caught a large, plump rabbit.

"I've learned to set a snare just as well as Sabattis," Brad thought. He would be proud to show this fine rabbit to Sabattis' father. They would eat well tonight.

Brad picked up the rabbit. He had started back to the cabin when he heard a shout from the river.

"Hello there! Hello there!" called a deep, strong voice.

14

Together Again

The voice sent a thrill up Brad's spine. It was so like his father's voice. So very like. But it could not be. Not after all this time. Brad ran toward the river. He saw two canoes fast approaching the shore. In one was a strange white man and two small forms huddled in the bottom of the canoe. A woman with the hood of a dark cape over her head was in the bow of the other canoe. Another white man was paddling from near the stern. Brad stared at the man and woman, excitement growing in him. They looked familiar. Yet Brad still could not be sure.

Now the canoes were closer. "Hello, there, Indian!" called the same familiar voice. "We come as friends."

And now Brad knew that this man was his father. And the woman in the cape must be his mother. His family had come at last.

"Pa! Ma!" Brad waded into the shallows up to his waist. The thin skim of ice over the water cracked and tinkled like broken glass. Brad did not even feel the shock of the icy water. He seized the bow of the canoe and pulled it ashore.

"No, it can't be. It's no Indian. It's Brad!" cried his mother, almost falling as she stepped from the canoe. But in a minute she was hugging him. "Thank God! Thank God you're here alive. Oh, Brad, I worried so about you!"

"I saw you on the bank and thought you were an Indian," said Brad's father. "I never expected to see you alive." His voice broke with emotion.

Now Brad and his father were helping the other canoe land. Brad held the canoe steady and the strange man who had been paddling lifted two little girls, one after the other, ashore. They were so thin and pale Brad hardly recognized his little sisters.

"Hello, Prudy. Hello, Trudy," he said.

The little girls backed away from him. They ran to their mother.

"Don't let the Injun scalp me," cried Prudy.

"I'm scared of him," cried Trudy.

166

Brad stared at the man and the woman in the canoe

"He's no Indian. He's your brother Brad," said Mrs. Porter.

"I must say he fooled me. He looks more like an Injun than many of them critters I've seen. Real Injuns, I mean," said the man Brad did not know.

Something about the way he spoke offended Brad. "Don't you call them critters. Indians are better than many white men. I wouldn't be alive today if the Indians hadn't saved my life. They're the best friends I've ever had." Brad spoke angrily.

"Now don't speak that way to Jim Fenton," said Brad's father, beginning to unload the canoe. "I hired him to help move us up river and he's been a tower of strength. If Indians were good to you, Brad, I'll always be in their debt. Now help unload. Better run up to the cabin with Prudy and Trudy," he told his wife. "Best get them in out of the cold."

Suddenly, in the midst of his happiness at seeing his family safe and sound, Brad felt a surge of resentment.

"Why didn't you come before?" he asked his father. "I nearly starved to death. Why didn't you come when you said you would?"

"You mustn't blame your father," said Brad's mother quickly. "When he got back to Boston he found us all sick with black typhoid. He had to help take care of us, and then he caught it and nearly died. It was weeks and

168

weeks before his fever went down and when it did it left him weak as a rag. He's hardly strong enough to come now, but he would do it."

"I came just as soon as I was able," said Mr. Porter.

Brad saw that his father's face was pale and thin. It showed he had been ill. "I guess I knew you would have come if you could," Brad said.

Cold though it was, Brad's mother did not go to the cabin ahead of the menfolks. "I can't bear to have you out of my sight," she told Brad. She stood with a little girl wrapped in each side of her full wool skirt and watched the unloading of the canoes.

There were barrels and blankets and sacks. Carefully wrapped glass for the cabin window. One small rocking chair, the only piece of furniture Mrs. Porter had brought from her old home. It looked strange up here in the woods, Brad thought.

Everyone carried something up to the cabin. Even each of the little girls took a quilt. Brad carried a heavy firkin of lard easily. "You've grown strong," said his father. "Six months ago you couldn't have lifted that off the ground."

"I can lug things heavier than this," said Brad, as he walked along beside his father. "Why, Sabattis and I brought home a whole deer together. We must have carried it nearly a mile."

Unthinkingly, Brad spoke in Indian language. He had been speaking Indian so long that it came as naturally to him as his native tongue.

"Guess you'll have to speak English if you want me to understand you," said his father. "You must have been with Indians a long time to have learned their language."

Then Brad told his father how he and Sabattis had lived together all summer and autumn. He had not finished telling half what had happened, when they reached the cabin.

"They're in there now, Sabattis and his father, Chief Kineowa," said Brad. He was suddenly doubtful how his white family and his Indian family would get along together.

"Good! Then I'll have a chance to thank them for their great kindness to you. It's a kindness I shall never be able to repay," said Brad's father.

"They're going to adopt me," said Brad and then stopped, his hand halfway to the latch of the cabin door. For he realized that now that his white family had come, there was no need for him to go to live with the Indians. And that would mean that he would be separated from Sabattis, his brother, as dear to him as a blood brother.

"Hurry up and let us in, son. We're cold. This trip has been a long, hard pull for us all," said Mr. Porter.

Brad flung the door open.

"Here's my folks, come at last," he said loudly. Then, realizing he had spoken in English, he repeated his words in Indian.

At the sight of strangers, Chief Kineowa had sprung to his feet. Sabattis had raised the big wooden spoon from the stewpot and stood with it, ready to strike if he needed to.

As he heard Brad's words, Chief Kineowa's stern expression softened and the fierceness went out of his eyes.

"You have been a long time on the way," he said politely.

Brad's father put down the two heavy sacks he was carrying. He greeted Chief Kineowa with outstretched hand. "The Porter family can never thank you enough," he said. "Tell him that, Brad. Tell him that as long as I live I shall never forget how kind he and his son have been to you."

Even before Brad translated his father's words, the Indian chief seemed to understand their meaning. The two men clasped hands firmly. Beside the Indian, Brad's father looked frail and thin.

Now Brad's mother, his little sisters, and Jim Fenton came in. The little girls hid behind their mother's skirts and peered out at the Indians. Mrs. Porter smiled at them. "Anyone who has been good to my son is my friend," she said sincerely.

171

Brad saw his mother look at the soot-encrusted kettle. She coughed as the wind blew down the chimney hole and sent smoke swirling into the cabin. In spite of her long hard trip, she looked neat as a pin. It occurred to Brad that his mother's soul of neatness might be offended by the unswept cabin floor, the raccoon skins flung in the corner, and the musty blankets and deerskins on the bunk. Brad had not noticed the disorder until he saw her look around.

"Guess Sabattis and I didn't keep things very ship-shape," he said.

Brad's mother's eyes shone; her whole face was smiling. "Now that we're all together again it seems like home," she said. And Brad suddenly had a feeling of home and togetherness as a family that he had almost forgotten. He would have been perfectly happy if Sabattis had not stood apart, scowling. His mouth looked sullen and his eyes full of resentment. He was not glad Brad's family had come. He looked as if he were sorry they were still alive.

15

Between Two Magnets

Supper was a strange meal. Mrs. Porter put a red-and-white checked tablecloth on the floor in front of the fireplace, and they all sat around it. She dished some of the stew onto tin plates for herself and the little girls. Then the others reached into the pot with their fingers. Brad sensed that his father did this out of courtesy to the Indians.

Chief Kineowa ate heartily. Sabattis, who usually enjoyed his food, ate little. He haughtily refused a piece of cheese Mrs. Porter offered him. He would not even take a lump of maple sugar, although he had once told Brad that he was fond of it. Brad knew he was jealous. "He should know that the family's coming won't make me think any less of him," Brad thought. But in his heart he was not sure. For months Sabattis had been all the family he had. Now he had other ties of affection. What that would mean to his relationship with Sabattis, Brad did not know. He was still excited and confused.

"You look like an Injun but you really are Brad," said Prudy, snuggling up to him.

"Really are Brad," echoed Trudy, leaning on the other side.

The little girls had rediscovered their big brother under his Indian disguise.

"I know a place in the woods that's like a little room," Brad told them. "There are walls of trees all around, but inside is an empty place with just room enough for you to play house. In summer it has a floor of the greenest moss — like a velvet carpet."

"Take us to see it now," pleaded both little girls.

"It's too dark tonight. Tomorrow," Brad promised. Then he remembered that he had expected to leave with the Indians the next morning. If he went with them, he would be abandoning his own family. If he stayed with the family, he would have to watch Sabattis go without him. He felt torn between two loyalties.

Mrs. Porter had brought out two brass candlesticks, which she had placed on the shelf above the fireplace. The tongues of flame from bayberry candles were pretty,

Brad thought. He had not seen candlelight since he had used up his last candle in July. Sabattis and he had made torches of closely rolled birch bark soaked in grease and fastened to sticks. Most evenings, firelight had been enough. Now the candles lighted up the Indian chief's strong features, but the glow of firelight seemed a more appropriate lighting for Chief Kineowa's strong, bronzed face.

"I wish you to tell your father what I have in my mind," the chief said to Brad. "Tell him that you have become as a brother to my son." Chief Kineowa went on speaking, and Brad listened closely. Then he interpreted the chief's words.

"He says," Brad told his father, "that when he and Sabattis found me I was nearly starved. He says that if they had not taken care of me my soul would soon have left my body. (And he's right, Pa.) He says that I was like a small child, knowing nothing about how to live in the forest until Sabattis taught me. (And that's true enough.) He says that I can now hunt and fish as well as an Indian. (And I have become pretty good, though maybe not quite as good as Sabattis.) And Chief Kineowa says," and here Brad's voice faltered slightly, "that Sabattis is now my brother. That it is as if we were two branches of the same tree; that I am a grafted branch but will be just as close to him. He says that it will hurt us both if

Sabattis and I are separated." Brad paused and swallowed hard. "He says Sabattis has always wanted a brother and now he has found me. (I've always wanted a brother, too, Pa.) "

"Go on. What else did Chief Kineowa say?" asked Mr. Porter.

"He says," and Brad's voice was low, "that they want to adopt me into their tribe, the bear tribe. (That's a great honor, Pa.) They will call me He-who-runs-like-the-wind, because I kept up with Sabattis when we ran down a moose."

"Is that all?" asked Mr. Porter.

"Yes, Pa. I was going to go with them in the morning. I was going to live with the Indians."

"And are you?" asked Mr. Porter. "I won't lift a finger to stop you if you really want to go."

"But you can't go. Your father needs you," cried Mrs. Porter, her eyes anxious.

"It's not a question of need. I won't deny I could use Brad's help, but I can manage without it if I have to. He owes a great deal to these Indians. If he prefers to go to live with them, I won't hold him here," said Brad's father.

In the glow of the firelight and candles, Brad looked at the faces of those he loved. They were of two races, of two different ways of life, and he could not belong to both. It was like feeling the strong pull of opposing magnets. He had to give up one; go all the way to one or the other.

Brad was not long in making the choice that he had to make.

"Oh, Sabattis," his thoughts said, "I hate to let you go without me, but I must. I shall miss you. I shall be lonely without you." Part of Brad wanted to go with the Indians but more of him belonged to his white family. He felt in his very bones that this was so, even while he grieved at being separated from Sabattis.

"I shall stay with my white family," he told the Indians, and he saw the stricken expression in Sabattis' eyes, before the sullen look came into them again.

"What did you tell them?" asked Brad's mother anxiously.

"What did you expect me to tell them?" asked Brad. "If I'm not an orphan, why should I be adopted?"

He spoke again to the Indians and tried to explain why he could not come with them. It was difficult to find words.

"I understand," said Chief Kineowa. "The bond of blood is strong."

"Oh, Brad, for a minute you frightened me," said his mother.

"Did he make a face at you?" asked Prudy.

"He made up his mind," said Mr. Porter gravely, "and there are a few times in a man's life when that is the most difficult thing he will ever be called upon to do."

The little girls were tired and sleepy. Their mother took the boys' blankets and deerskins off the bunk, and Jim Fenton helped her put a featherbed on it. She tucked the children in under homespun blankets. "Sleep tight," she told them.

"Will we be here in the morning?" asked Trudy, a little fearful of the strangeness.

"Of course we'll be here," said Prudy. "It's our new home, isn't it, Ma?"

Mrs. Porter heard the wind howl outside. She looked toward the hearth and saw the two Indians squatting before the fire. The firelight shone on the dirt floor. Even this dim light revealed the bareness of the cabin. She sighed. Then her eyes fell on Brad, who sat beside his father, and she said cheerfully, "Yes, it's our new home and we'll be happy here. Now say your prayers and go to sleep. And don't forget to thank God that your brother Brad is safe and well. We have a great deal to be thankful for."

Back at the fireside, Mr. Porter and Jim Fenton began to unpack some of the Porter belongings. Mr. Porter offered Chief Kineowa his choice of gifts. "You and Sabattis take anything I have and I'll still be indebted to you," he told Brad to tell them. And he showed them a great cake of maple sugar, a round cart wheel of yellow cheese, a ten-gallon jug of molasses, a sack of hand-wrought nails, a larger sack of dried pea beans, a big slab of salt pork, a good-sized pile of dried codfish. Then he unpacked something that caught Brad's eye — two rifles, one of them brand new — as beautiful a shooting iron as he had ever laid eyes on.

"Take anything except the new rifle," Mr. Porter told Chief Kineowa. "That I brought to Brad."

Brad took the beautiful gun in his hands. Its metal parts gleamed in the firelight. It was something any boy would be proud to own. A little earlier Brad had told his father about the rifle he had lost in the woods the day the cow moose had chased him. Yet his father had not reproached him. He was giving him this handsome rifle just the same. Brad had always longed for a rifle of his own.

Then Brad saw that Sabattis was also admiring the rifle. Brad remembered that Sabattis had shared his steel-tipped arrows with him. He remembered the long months of their companionship.

"Take it. It's yours," Brad said, and he put the rifle into Sabattis' hands. "Pa gave it to me, so it's mine to give. I want you to have it."

There were signs of a struggle in Sabattis' face. Then,

for the first time since the arrival of Brad's family, he lost his look of sullen anger.

"I accept it. I shall take the most careful ownership of this fine rifle," he said. "I thank my white brother."

All Chief Kineowa would accept was the cake of maple sugar and one blanket.

"The bear tribe is not poor," he said, "but I will not refuse gifts from friends."

Then Chief Kineowa told Brad that even though he was not coming to live with the bear tribe, he was still welcome to visit them. "When the water of the river is stilled and the snow deep upon it," he said, "Sabattis will come for you on snowshoes. He will bring snowshoes for you and, if your father permits, you and he will walk up river to our island village. There we will have ceremonies around the campfire and adopt you into our tribe. Even though you live apart from us, He-who-runs-like-the-wind will always be welcome to sit at the campfire of the bear tribe."

In a rush of words, Brad told his father what the chief had said. "May I go? May I?" Brad asked eagerly.

"I see no reason why you can't visit your Indian friends," said Brad's father. "As soon as we get things shipshape around the cabin, you'll be free to go. Tell that to the chief. And tell him that he and Sabattis and any member of the bear tribe will always be welcome guests in our home."

Everyone except the little girls was up before daylight the next morning. There were to be two departures. Jim Fenton was taking his canoe downstream, and the Indians would paddle theirs upstream. Although they all wanted to start early, Mrs. Porter insisted that they first eat a hearty breakfast.

181

As they sat near the fire, eating, Chief Kineowa said, "In two nights the moon will show its full face. Then the river will be stilled and the ice deep, and canoes must rest until spring."

When Brad had interpreted the chief's words, Mr. Porter said, "Lucky for you, Jim, that going downstream is quicker than coming up, or you wouldn't make it to Bangor before the river freezes. Lucky I got here when I did. Another few days and I couldn't have reached here until spring."

When Brad told the chief what his father had said, Chief Kineowa nodded.

"Your father speaks true," the chief said to Brad. "Tell him that I know now it was the will of the Great Spirit that you remain his son. If the Great Spirit had meant it otherwise, the river would have frozen deep sooner."

Sabattis seemed to agree with his father. He no longer looked sullen. He kept the rifle near at hand while he ate. He had looked with suspicion at the flapjacks Mrs. Porter had made for breakfast, but when he had eaten one, with golden molasses poured over it, he accepted four more and still four more.

"Tell him they would have been better if I had had milk to put in them," Brad's mother said.

"They taste plenty good to me," said Brad, taking

another. After so many months of Indian cooking, they tasted wonderful.

Brad and his father went out to see Jim Fenton and the Indians leave. Jim left first. He was a slow-spoken man who hoarded words. He had not spoken more than a dozen sentences since he had arrived. He had done what he had been hired to do, help get the Porter family here. He had not been paid to talk. Now, as he stepped into his canoe, he said, "See you next spring, Mr. Porter, if you're still alive by then."

Jim Fenton pushed off from shore with his paddle and soon was paddling swiftly downstream, the current helping him along.

Brad did not mind seeing Jim go. It was hard, though, to watch Sabattis and his father take their places in their canoe. Sabattis, his rifle beside him, was in the bow. There were no words of farewell spoken. Everything needful had been said.

The two Indians picked up their paddles. Brad and his father pushed the canoe away from the riverbank. Resting his paddle an instant, Chief Kineowa raised his arm in a gesture of friendship and farewell. Sabattis made no sign. He went in silence without another look at Brad. Perhaps he, like Brad, had tears in his eyes.

Brad and his father stood on the dead grass along the riverbank and looked up river until the Indians' canoe was out of sight. Ice had formed at the edge of the leaden river. The November wind was cutting. Brad saw his father hunch his thin shoulders against it.

"Brad," said his father, "I want to tell you that I know how you feel. There's something in every last man of us that longs to be perfectly free. Perhaps the Indian way of life is as free a life as any. To have no responsibilities beyond fishing and hunting would be to live a life of eternal boyhood. It may be good for the Indians, Brad, but it's not good for you. You have to grow up; become a man."

"You can't call Chief Kineowa a boy. He's a man," said Brad.

"Yes, he's every inch a man," agreed his father. "It was not fair to the Indians to speak as I did. Their way of life is different from ours, but there are big men among them. Big men in more than one way. Chief Kineowa is one of the best. I can't blame you for being tempted to go to live with him and Sabattis."

"I never really considered it, not after you and Ma and the twins came," said Brad stoutly. "Honest, I didn't."

"Come right down to it," said Mr. Porter, "if you had, I don't know how I would have gotten on without you."

His father did need him, Brad realized, yet he had left him free to make his own choice. That was one of the reasons Brad could not have chosen otherwise than

the way he had. His father was not a man who leaned. He could stand alone if he had to. But Brad knew his young strength would be a most welcome help.

Brad had chosen, and would not repent of his choice. He would stay and help his father tame his savage acres, cut down trees, make pasture land and garden — hack a farm from the Maine wilderness. He would do all this willingly. Yet all the time something in him would be wanting to leave the forest untouched except by the seasons and the weather.

Often at night when he looked up at the stars, Brad would search for the constellation of the Great Bear, the guiding stars of the bear tribe. And he would think of how he and Sabattis had run with the moose together through the wild woods. He would remember days when they had been as much a part of the forest as any wild creature who lived there. He would never forget his Indian brother.

Author's Note

Several years ago while doing research about the War of 1812, I came upon a brief mention of a boy who had gone up the Penobscot River with his father. The boy had been left in the woods alone while his father had gone back to Massachusetts for the rest of the family. The father was delayed in returning to Maine, and the boy would have starved if he had not been befriended by Indians.

Just these bare facts were given, and since this part of one paragraph had nothing to do with the subject I was looking up, I did not even make note of the book it was in. I remember only that it was in a book about the State of Maine. But I never forgot that there had been such a boy. I kept wondering what had really happened while he was alone in the wilderness, what he was like, what sort of man was his father, and what Indians befriended him and how. I kept imagining things about him. Finally, after doing a great deal of reading about the time in which he had lived, after consulting all the books I could find about the Penobscot Indians, and after visiting the Indian Reservation at Old Town, I wrote the story about what I think could have happened.

I do not know, but it could have been that the real boy's father moved from Massachusetts to Maine for the same reason Brad's did: he was out of work because of the embargo on shipping. In the year 1809, even coastwise shipping was against the law for three months, a time of great hardship for Boston and other ports. Soon after the embargo was imposed in 1807, unemployed seamen and shipbuilders began to leave the seaports and move inland. By 1809, thousands had left Massachusetts. Some went to Ohio; others, like Brad's father, bought uncleared land in Maine.

Bangor was already a town in 1809. Old Town, thirteen miles up river from Bangor, had a few white settlers but was mostly Indian reservation. It took courage for a white man to settle on land up river from Old Town, for the Indians believed that the forests along the river belonged to them. The Indians felt that they had often been deprived of their land unjustly. They no longer made war on the whites in Maine, but a lone settler might have been in danger from them.

An Indian reservation still exists at Old Town. It is on an island in the Penobscot now connected with the mainland by a bridge. When I visited the reservation I met a small boy who said he belonged to the bear family, though his family now goes by the name of Mitchell. I found names of Indian chiefs in the old island cemetery and the graves of men who were alive when far more than this tiny part of Maine belonged to the Penobscot Indians.

H.W.